THE PERFECT SPECIMEN

M. LUKE MCDONELL

The Perfect Specimen is a work of fiction. Names, characters, places, and incidents are either products of the author's imagination or used fictitiously. Any resemblance to actual persons, places or incidents is entirely coincidental.

Copyright © 2013 by M. Luke McDonell

http://www.mlukemcdonell.com

ISBN: 978-0-9912153-2-4

This novella is dedicated to the fearless readers of my early drafts. I was advised to try to find one "perfect reader," but I found so many more. Your enthusiasm, comments, and critiques shaped this work. Thank you so much!

Celia Breslin, Julie Chiron, Diana Coffa, Lorelei David, Rusty Hodge, Susan Jennings, Todd Jordan, David Kuehn, Michael Koperwas, Laura LaGassa, Dave LaMacchia, Ted Leibowitz, Lamont Lucas, Jennifer Lynch, Dawn Newton, Nancee McDonell, Daniele Mills, Mary-Mignon Mitchell, Hiroshi Morisaki, Rachel Perkins, Alicia Pollak, Frederick Roeber, Alex Rosenberg, Gina Sanfilipo, Patricia Schoenstein, Jennifer Waggoner, Sasha Vodnik, and Allison Yates.

Thanks to Amelia Peace for her portrayal of Mia on the cover.

A special thanks to http://www.somafm.com for providing the perfect soundtrack for writing.

Chapter One

The double-paned glass front doors of the Han University Annex slid open and hot, acrid air pressed against the front of my body like a warning hand. Reflexively, I took a step back, then pushed myself out of the air-conditioned cocoon and into the real world.

The walkway to the street was covered, but it was late in the day and thin hot beams of sunlight slipped between the columns and scored my path. After only a few steps, I was panting. The air was painfully dry and although the city was built on a completely flat plain, the above Earth-standard gravity made me feel I was perpetually climbing stairs.

Despite that, I usually walked home from work. I needed the exercise after spending nine hours on a cushioned chair doing little more than wiggling my fingers. On the days I tested the drug, though, I needed to get to the privacy of my apartment as quickly as possible. I always printed the drug with an extra-thick capsule so I'd have time to get out of the building without activating the scanners, but I kept my eyes down as I hurried through the long hallways, worried that I'd botched the formula and the gleaming white marble floor might be about to liquefy.

I hailed a pod and climbed in.

"Good afternoon Dr. Singh. Where would you like to go?" the pod asked in a melodic, vaguely female voice. I wondered if women passengers were greeted by a man.

I slid across the slick white plastic seat and peered out the left window. "Home," I commanded. No need to give my address. I was in the Han sector and everything here knew everything about me. The door clicked shut and we eased into the quiet, orderly flow of vehicles that people on this planet laughably called rush hour.

As usual, the idiot pod was taking me on yet another tour of New Canberra. The city engineers explained this as "traffic management." I called it irritating. I was sure there was a way to specify my preferred route, but even after seven months in the city I had a hard time wading through the masses of data available on my glasses.

We hummed past gleaming new high-rises, rolled down perfect residential streets, plowed through the advertising holos that spanned the road in the shopping district and veered to avoid bristling construction sites. The Han Corporation's cartoonish attempts to make this sector as Earthlike as possible failed; the landscaping and architecture only accentuated the alien environment. The buildings to my left and right could have been plucked from any nouveau riche African city, but the bright blue-green sky was a color stolen from a neon sign and dialed up to such intensity I couldn't look at it without my glasses set on dark. The sun–too big and too yellow–coated more than illuminated, and the drooping jacaranda trees lining the streets struggled to stay upright under the weight of the thick honey light. The benches and paths on the wide, center median were nothing but set pieces on a planet where the daytime temperature never dropped below 35˚C.

Despite all the detours, I made it home with ten minutes to spare.

I paced the length of my nearly empty living room with the anxiety of a host waiting for the first party guest to arrive. For me it was a question of what, not who, would visit itself upon me tonight.

I didn't notice my feet going numb until I stumbled. Crap. Too much sedative. When my hands started to tingle, I gave up and lay down on one of the few pieces of furniture in the room—an unfashionably puffy orange sofa I'd rescued from a trip down the recycling chute. I stared at the ceiling and wondered once again why I was neglecting research that could help millions to save one little girl.

I was napping when my wall screen chimed.

"Della Singh." The speakers that ringed the apartment chorused my wife's name.

Why was she calling now? I glanced at the section of my interactive wall that displayed the date and time in Austin and New Canberra. Austin, 3 a.m., March 15, 2121, and above it, New Canberra, 6:30 p.m., Sommer 18, VY 15. Della was usually in bed by 10 p.m.

"Accept," I called out as I pushed myself to a seated position with wooden block hands.

Della jittered into existence. The crummy laser scanner we had at home sent a version of her little better than an amateur pointillist painting. Brown slashes for hair, a flat white face, and polka dot eyes the wrong shade of blue.

"Hey babe, why are you up so late?" I asked.

"Quiet!" she admonished. "Jeremy has a cold. I just got him to sleep."

I tried not to frown. She controlled the volume of my voice in the house, not me.

"You didn't come home last night," she stated.

Her wavering pixilated eyes were angry. The laser was badly calibrated and I pitied the man half a meter to my right who was receiving the bulk of her wrath.

We'd both applied for the prestigious two-year research grant. I knew I wouldn't be selected but Della insisted it would look bad if I didn't try. All the big players in my specialty–medicinal uses of arthropod venom–were on Victoria.

I wasn't a big player though. I wasn't a player at all. My PhD thesis was full of revolutionary ideas, all of which failed to produce any positive results in the 10 years since I'd been hired by the university. My department head made it clear that although he didn't expect me to personally cure cancer, if I didn't make some progress soon he'd have to give my spot to a more promising recent graduate.

Della panicked. She was on tenure-track and committed to the University of Texas. In her mind, a two-professor, two-income household was the paved highway to our future. I'd only recently realized I wasn't the one driving.

No one was more shocked than I when my name was read as the grant winner. My first thought was that my coworkers had played a cruel joke on me. I forced a chuckle and congratulated them. Their confused faces and the elaborate holographic certificate my boss held wiped the smile from my face.

Shit.

Jeremy was two and a half and finally getting interesting. Della and I had just bought our first house and I'd planted apple and peach trees in the backyard. The spindly sticks would be producing fruit by the time I got back and Jeremy would be a completely different person–one who might not even recognize me.

I did not want to go to Victoria.

Della, elated, practically thumbed the "accept" button for me. To her, this was a vindication; my research did have promise and UT couldn't fire me. She swore that taking care of Jeremy on her own for two years wouldn't be a problem. I knew her better than that. She'd push herself until she cracked, and apparently, tonight was that night.

"I was at the lab," I told her. It was easier to work on my special project when my assistant wasn't around.

"No, you weren't. When you didn't pick up your L-chat, I called the front desk and they said you checked out at 6 p.m."

I tried to glare but my eyebrows weren't fully functional yet. "I don't accept calls after six. That's what 'checked out' means."

"You're drunk."

I sighed and slumped back into the couch. I wanted to tell her what I was doing, to explain everything, but I couldn't afford the triple-encrypted gray-market link I'd need to ensure our conversation wasn't recorded and analyzed. Drunk was a good explanation for my state, so I agreed.

"Maybe a little. I miss you and Jeremy." I looked out the glass doors. "You should see the stars here Della. They're amazing."

For a moment she relented and her face relaxed into that of the pretty, inquisitive woman I fell in love with. "I wish I could. Are you okay? You look tired."

I shrugged, but I suspected the gesture wasn't of high enough resolution to make it back to Earth. "I'm still not used to the gravity."

Della turned her head before I heard the muffled cry. Jeremy was awake.

She stood. "I have to go."

I stumbled to my feet and our ghosts faced each other. "I won't be home tomorrow night. Wanna talk Saturday morning? 10 a.m. your time?"

Her voice broke up as she walked out of range of the scanner. "I'll try. It depends on Jeremy."

The bright white pixels of her receding back winked out.

I flopped back down onto the couch. Della was one of the best scientists I knew, and her unspoken hypothesis was that I was cheating.

The irony was that there was another woman, but she was nine years old.

Chapter Two

A few months ago, I was doing what I always did after work–sipping an ice cold beer and watching the last rays of the setting sun slide up the distant mountains. I'd had another frustrating day. When I won the grant, I assumed I'd not only have access to all of Han's expensive, state-of-the-art equipment but also to the venom I'd need for my cancer research. It turned out the competition was even fiercer here than on Earth and my fellow scientists didn't share data or anything else. I was limited to extracting venom from whatever I could catch in the nearby undeveloped land, and I wasn't catching much.

Mia, the kid who lived next door, leapt out onto her balcony and slammed the door shut behind her.

"Hi Derek!" Her blue eyes lit up and she gave me a big, snaggle-toothed smile. She was literally the only person on the planet consistently happy to see me. Her blonde-streaked brown hair was tangled and dusty and she wore tan coveralls–standard protection against sun and poisonous creatures. The smallest adult size was much too large for her petite, nine-year old frame. Victoria was not a place for children and the only ones here were the sons and daughters of the first wave of engineers and executives that settled the planet.

It'd taken a while for us to become friends. At first, she'd run inside whenever I came out. After a few weeks, she'd stay outside but reply to my salutations with only a quizzical gaze. Eventually curiosity got the better of her and she started grilling me. Once she found out I studied "bugs" she decided I was okay. I tried to explain that insects were only one class of arthropod and what she was seeing out in the desert included chilopods, diplopods, arachnids, and many others, but she was quick to correct my mistake. Everything out there was a bug.

She hopped closer to my balcony. I envied her obliviousness to the gravity that pressed me down onto any available horizontal surface as firmly as an iron flattening a wrinkled shirt. I dragged the padded lounge chair to face her and succumbed.

"Hi Mia. You been out playing behind the building?"

"No. I took a pod to the big rocks at 17th and Avenue A and there was..."

She broke off, her eyes unfocused. I suspected she had a developmental or learning disorder or had a head injury when she was younger. She'd often stop talking mid-sentence and get the vacant-eyed look she had now. When she spoke again it might be about a completely different subject. Other times, she'd talk about things she saw that weren't there–unusual clouds, a sculpture on my balcony that must have belonged to the former tenant–all in present tense and great detail. After I got over my initial confusion, this didn't bother me. My department at the University of Texas was filled with self-proclaimed geniuses; awkward pauses and non sequiturs were part of any discussion. Whatever was wrong with Mia, she wasn't stupid.

"How was school today?" I prompted. A question usually brought her back.

She dangled her arms over the glass railing. "Okay. Boring."

I took another sip of beer. "Why boring?"

She flapped her arms against the glass, making clean streaks. "I can't talk and I can't wear my glasses. There's nothing to do."

"You don't use glasses?"

She shook her head and let her hair fall over her face. "No. We aren't allowed. We have desk screens and the teacher controls them. Boring, boring, boring." She kicked a pot of wilted bamboo to emphasize this.

I relaxed as the beer made its way from my empty stomach into my bloodstream. Mia chattered on about school. It was too bad she had to spend so much time by herself. Her parents worked late every night and it was obvious she was lonely. When I'd asked if she ever played with friends, she glared, and I remembered how cruel children could be to those that didn't fit in.

When she paused, I broke in. "Hey Mia, my department is having an open house tomorrow evening. You want to come? You can see real specimens, not just holos." Once a quarter all the labs opened their doors to spouses and kids for an informal show and tell.

She held onto the top of the railing and let her legs go limp, dangling. "I know all the bugs."

I laughed. "You might know the ones around here but we have a huge library from all of Han's territory." That I wasn't allowed to touch, I silently added. I pointed vaguely north. "You haven't been to the poles, have you?"

She hung, and her eyes got that strange unfocused look they often did. "The poles...the top and bottom of Victoria?"

"Yep. There are some really unusual creatures there."

A drone slowed its flight to examine us. This happened whenever I was on my balcony and it irritated the shit out of me. New Canberra had more security in one square kilometer than I'd seen in all of Austin and though I knew that I had no privacy on the streets or at work, I was supposed to have it at home. It was in the contract: Han monitoring stopped at my front door. This loophole, spying from outside, violated the spirit of the agreement, yet no one else seemed bothered by this. Yes, I understood that the planet had only been settled 15 years ago and that "anything could happen," but the idea that the ubiquitous drones were here to protect us from a swarm of insects was preposterous.

Mia frowned. "You'll have to ask my mom if I can go. I don't know if it is age appropriate."

I snorted. "Kids are welcome. I'll ask her tonight when I get back."

Mia gave a wiggly shrug and went indoors with no goodbye. I tilted my head back and drained my beer. It was almost time for me to set my traps. The golden tips of the mountains faded to gray as the sun set into the Western sea and I got the surge of energy I got every day at this hour. Time to take off the lab coat and the professional demeanor and go play in the dirt.

Chapter Three

I'd never formally met the Julians. No one in the building was very friendly. I exchanged nods with the people I met in the lobby or passed in the hall, but the camaraderie I expected to find amongst people living on an alien planet did not exist. Everyone was too busy to socialize outside of work. I'd found the southern hospitality in Austin as overwhelming as the humidity. Now, I missed both.

Mr. Julian was a civil engineer, and his wife, Dr. Julian, was a mechanical engineer. After months as neighbors, that was all I knew about them.

I knocked on their door, aware I was breaking an unspoken rule. Mr. Julian answered, his face showing polite confusion. Unannounced guests were a rare occurrence in a building like ours.

"Yes?"

I stuck out my hand. "Hey there. I'm Derek Singh. I live next door."

He stared at me a few moments longer, then broke into the same crooked grin I was used to seeing on Mia. "Oh, right! I'm Matthew."

He was in his mid 40's with wavy, dark hair peppered with gray. His brown eyes were friendly but still quizzical.

"I work at the university annex. We're having an open house tomorrow evening. I thought Mia might be interested in coming. You are welcome, too," I quickly added.

He raised his eyebrows. "You know Mia?"

His wife came up behind him and regarded me coolly. She was a tall woman with long brown hair and an angular face more architectural than pretty. Her mouth was wide and downturned and emanated disapproval. Mia had gotten her sky blue eyes from her and fortunately, little else.

I gestured to the windows at the far end their large, spare living room. "We both spend time on the balcony in the afternoon."

Dr. Julian's frown deepened and I hurried to explain. "Mia on your balcony and me on mine. They're only half a meter apart."

Mia's mother gave her husband a sharp look.

"We haven't met. I'm Derek."

"I didn't realize the previous tenant had moved out. I'm Dr. Julian. Annette." She didn't offer her hand, but stood aside. "Please, come in."

I edged past her and settled uncomfortably on the middle section of a long blocky couch. Mr. and Dr. Julian sat across from me. The low stone table that separated us was bare but for a beautifully-trained bonsai tree in a green-glazed pot.

Mia bounded in, breaking the awkward silence. "Derek! You are in my house!"

"I am. I'm telling your parents about the open house at the Annex tomorrow night."

Mia looked at her mother uneasily, as if worried she'd done something wrong, then went to nestle beside her father.

He hugged her before turning to me. "I'm sorry we haven't met before now. We work more than we should. How long will you be here? 10-year contract?"

"No," I said, "two-year research grant. Not much time to get anything done. How about you?"

"We're in it for the long haul. When Mia was born we signed 30-year contracts. It is almost impossible for kids born on Victoria to immigrate to Earth. You heard about that?"

I shook my head.

"The Associated Governments of Earth are irritated that Victoria hasn't opened its doors to the unwashed masses. In retaliation they won't grant residency to anyone born here. Student visas are all they issue. If we move back, Mia can't come with us."

Annette broke in. "You said you're doing research at the university annex. What are you studying?" She reminded me of the older, uptight professors at UT: officious and demanding.

"The cytolytic properties of arthropod venom. I'm hoping to find a venom that can be modified to only destroy cancerous tumors. I'm lucky to be here. All of the cutting edge work is being done on Victoria," I said.

Matthew nodded and started to ask a question, but Annette interrupted. "Do you have children?" She'd noticed my ring.

"One, Jeremy. He's three." I patted my pocket, but I'd left the screen with family photos in my apartment.

"You have brothers and sisters?" she asked.

Her tone was more interrogative than friendly and Matthew and I both gave her a quizzical look.

"Two older brothers."

"You spend much time with children?" she asked.

"Not usually. In fact, I'd never held a baby until I held Jeremy."

"When did you meet Mia?" She watched me like my cat watched the holes under our house where the ground squirrels hid nuts.

This woman was beginning to irritate me. I wasn't a stalker. I'd befriended a lonely kid. "A few months ago."

Matthew laughed, comprehension dawning, and he poked Mia. "This is your friend Derek? The one you talk about?"

She nodded.

Matthew smiled broadly. "This clears up a big mystery. I couldn't figure out which of her classmates was the bug fanatic. I was starting to think you were a character from an educational immersion program."

"Go finish up your homework, Mia. The grownups need to talk," Annette said.

Mia snuggled closer to her father but he detached her and set her on her feet. "Go ahead sweetie. I'll play Sunspot with you later."

She shuffled out of the room. Annette started to speak but Matthew put a hand on her knee.

"Sorry to give you the third degree Derek. I'm sure the irony of this situation is obvious. We are very protective of our only child, yet we leave her alone, day after day."

He had an open, self-depreciating manner I liked. "I understand. I'm five weeks away from my son, and that's on a fast ship that I can't afford."

Matthew pointed to a silver ball hanging from the ceiling in the center of the room. "We try to keep an eye on Mia. I know the camera has a few blind spots." The right side of the balcony wasn't visible from the glass French doors.

I shrugged. "I don't think you need to worry. This city is the ultimate babysitter. Drones come by whenever we are out there. She's safer than any kid on Earth."

Annette nodded curtly. "That's true." She gave a thin, false smile. "I worry that Mia has been bothering you. She is very…imaginative. Has she been telling you any strange stories?"

This was her subtle attempt to acknowledge Mia's problem. I kept my face neutral. "Not really. She tells me a bit about everything and asks me lots of questions. She's a smart kid."

Annette continued. "She knows a lot of facts about things she is interested in. She has unusually good retention for a child her age."

I nodded in agreement, but wasn't going to be drawn in to a discussion of Mia's abilities and disabilities. "I'm sure she does, but as I said, I don't have a lot of data points. I haven't spent much time with kids. Mia and I have some fun chats. I thought she might like to come to the open house. If you don't want her to, that's fine."

She stiffened. "It isn't– "

Matthew rubbed his hand up and down her arm and she stopped speaking. Della and I had similar cues we used if one of us wanted to leave a party.

"Thanks for thinking of Mia," he said, "and I apologize for never stopping by to say hello. We don't know many people in the building anymore. We've been on Victoria for 12 years now and most of our friends have returned to Earth or moved to a better address near Ring One." He waved towards the star-studded blackness visible through the tall windows. "Not many people choose to live in the outer ring, but we like it."

"I do too. It's beautiful."

The majority of the population turned their backs on the too-vast emptiness and faced inward. I tried not to condemn them for this, but to travel all this way and then huddle around the transplanted green of Center Park was pathetic. Only in New Canberra would a high-floor apartment with an unobstructed view of the natural landscape rent for less than a lower-floor place that looked straight at the building next door.

We spent a moment in appreciation of the night, then I stood. "I need to get home. I'd be happy to show Mia around the lab tomorrow, and both of you as well if you can get away from work. I'll send you the details. No need to RSVP, just give my name at the front desk."

Matthew followed me to the door. "I'm glad we finally met." He smiled crookedly. "It doesn't surprise me that Mia's best friend is a 30-year old entomologist. She's a funny girl."

I corrected him. "36, and not an entomologist, an oncologist," and not Mia's best friend, I hoped.

Chapter Four

Mia did come to the open house, right on time, and with neither parent in tow. I caught sight of her in the central lab. She was backed up against the huge holo imaging machine, arms wrapped around her chest as she took quick, nervous looks up at the adults that surrounded her.

I was in the process of reprimanding my assistant, Anton. The university annex dress code was white lab coats, neck-high white shirts, dark gray pants and burgundy headbands, hats, or scarves. Han loved uniforms. I didn't mind. I'd only been allowed to bring 20 kilograms of luggage on this adventure and was glad it wasn't wasted on work clothes.

Anton wore his lab coat unbuttoned to below his sternum and nothing but tan skin beneath. He was a bad combination of young, cocky, and not very bright. I had no doubt his mother, a senior partner at Han, had gotten him this job to keep him out of trouble. Still, it irked me that I got fined if I so much as wore inappropriate shoes while Anton ambled through Han's prickly rules without a scratch.

"Hey there!" I greeted Mia, who'd appeared at my side.

She gave Anton and me the same suspicious once-over she'd been giving everyone else. "Where are all the bugs?" she demanded without preface.

"Right this way." I gave Anton a stern look and he smiled.

"I'm off the clock, boss. After 6 p.m. I can wear whatever I want."

Was there a time he couldn't? I'd like to be there. He snagged Emilia, a pretty intern, and the two of them pulled down their glasses and snaked their way towards the storage rooms in the back. Rooms he shouldn't be able to access now, but undoubtedly could.

I led Mia to the specimen display area. A floor to ceiling wall of glass cubes, each with a creature suspended within, ran the length of a 30-meter corridor. Any one of them might hold the key to destroying tumors without harming healthy flesh, but they were as off-limits to me as they were to the grubby toddlers that dragged greasy fingers across the smooth, unbreakable surfaces.

Mia unfolded her arms and gave a happy hop when she saw the bright squares and the nearest sample–a huge blue and green iridescent humming wasp from the south pole.

"What is that?"

I didn't get a chance to answer before another square caught her eye and her questions and observations tumbled excitedly over each other.

I pulled a pair of disposable glasses from the dispenser. "Use these. They only work on this wall and they will tell you everything you want to know and more."

My own glasses flashed an alert. I opened the results of my latest simulation. Tumor growth accelerated. Damn it. Sample 867, useless.

"Find me before you leave, okay? I have to work."

A few hours later as things were winding down, Mia skipped into the alcove that was my personal lab.

I was startled. I assumed she'd left long ago. Most kids ran around the bug wall for 10 minutes then wanted to play with the switches and buttons on the expensive equipment. When that was declared off-limits, tantrums ensued and the visit usually ended soon after.

"You still here? Won't your parents be worried?"

"My dad's gonna get me when he's done with work."

I glanced at a screen. He'd better come soon. At 8p.m. all non-employees would be escorted out. "Did you have a good time?"

She nodded seriously. "All the scientists really like Victoria."

"We're lucky to be here. There aren't many new things left to find on Earth."

Mia tugged shyly on my sleeve. It was the first time she'd touched me. "Come show me which bugs you like."

I let her pull me to the specimen wall, then took her to a spot in the middle and placed my finger on a square containing a seven-centimeter-long black line. "We have nothing like this on Earth. It has characteristics of both scorpions and centipedes–a segmented body with many legs, pincers, and a tail and stinger. The exoskeleton is very hard, and the eyes are very well developed. The pincers are strong and stingers very sharp–a necessary adaptation to prey which also have thick exoskeletons. The venom is very toxic–cytolytic actually. Do you know what that means?" I realized belatedly I'd gotten overly technical for a discussion with a nine-year old.

She shook her head.

"It destroys cells. I'm trying to find a venom that can be modified to destroy only tumors. No luck yet."

She wasn't paying much attention, instead looking intently at all the samples. "You don't have them all."

I laughed. "I hope not. We expect to find thousands more." Though, worryingly, this wasn't happening. I'd overheard the anxious conversations of the entomologists in the alcove next to mine. The chart showing the number of new species discovered each year was a bell curve, the current date somewhere near the bottom of the right side and heading down. The most deadly insects had no natural predators and could devour everything in a square kilometer in less than a month. The rumor hadn't made it back to Earth yet, but here in the lab, senior scientists suspected we'd found nearly all there was to find. I wasn't alarmed–I could spend several lifetimes analyzing the venom we already had–but Han Corporation funded our research and no partner would champion a division with no growth potential.

Mia pointed to a specimen near the floor. "I know one like this with stripes on the tail." She moved left. "And like this one, but it's yellow and speckled. And this one, but the front pincers are really big and the tail is smaller." She had her face pressed to the glass. "One like this but it has more eyes."

I listened with amused tolerance, certain she was combining bits of real creatures with those she'd seen in holos and educational programs. The extreme detail was the product of a child's imagination and desire to be helpful.

After she'd described 15 or so mythical creatures and was taking a breath to go on, I interrupted and began to ask detailed questions. How long? How many legs? How many segments in the body? She might tire of this game if I stymied her. I was happy to talk about real arthropods all day, but fiction of any sort didn't interest me.

She was happy to elaborate, but my intense questioning seemed to bring on a great number of her "spells." She'd pause before answering and her eyes would lose focus for a split second. I was sure if I waved my hand in front of her she wouldn't see. I didn't know if I should continue, but she didn't seem agitated or nervous and wasn't going off on any strange tangents like she sometimes did. I continued our game, but kept a hopeful eye out for her father.

When I asked her to tell me more about the front pincers of a particularly bizarre creature she'd invented, sudden suspicion flared in her eyes.

"This isn't a test, is it?" She said the word test with a mixture of fear and distaste.

I laughed. "God, no. Do you have verbal tests in school?"

She'd been sitting on the floor cross-legged; now she pulled her legs in to her chest and wrapped her arms around them. "No. We do them on screen. I hate tests. I don't understand them."

"They used to be worse. When I was a kid, it was all about memorizing, not understanding."

She looked at me quizzically. "Are you good at memorizing?"

"I'm okay, but I don't need to be with these." I tapped the glasses I'd pushed to the top of my head.

She made a funny, derisive sound and jumped up. "You want me to get you the bugs you don't have?"

I shook my head firmly. "No." I swept my arm to indicate the entire wall. "A sting or bite from most of these would make you very sick or kill you."

"I know Derek! I don't touch them with my bare hands. I used to catch them and make them fight each other. My dad made me stop. He said it was–"

"–Dangerous?" I supplied.

"No," she said petulantly. "Cruel. I don't see why though. They fight each other in the brush all the time."

How strange it must be to grow up on a planet with no animal life. Even pets from Earth were banned, though there was talk of allowing spayed and neutered cats and dogs.

"Would you like to learn more about these bugs?" Giving Mia something to do might make her long afternoons more enjoyable. "If your dad says it's okay, I'll give you a trap to try, but you have to promise to be careful. You can bring what you catch to me and I'll tell you all about it." Somewhere, distantly, my conscience twinged. I was encouraging a nine-year old to play with things that could kill her. Back home, someone who did this could expect a visit from child protective services. Mia had been out in the brush since she could walk, though, and god only knew how she caught bugs now.

Matthew appeared in the doorway as I was explaining a simple box trap to Mia and showing her the types of bait she could deploy. He was in coveralls and, except for a goggle-shaped patch of clean skin around his eyes, completely coated in fine, tan dust.

"Sorry I'm late! Thanks for keeping an eye on her," he said.

"No problem. She entertained herself."

Mia nodded gravely. "I saw new things."

He squeezed her shoulder. "I'm glad, honey."

"I'm going to lend Mia one of these if it's okay with you." I held up the trap. "I use it to catch land-dwelling arthropods and truthfully, I haven't had much luck. She says she can bring me all the bugs I don't have."

I expected him to smile–we were both in on the joke–but he nodded seriously. "I'm sure she can and I'd much rather have her bring them here than to her bedroom. You have to promise to be careful with this, Mia. This is scientific equipment, not a toy."

"I know." She held the gossamer box gently. "I'm going to be a research assistant."

Chapter Five

The next afternoon, the front desk security guard popped onto my screen, his face bemused. "Mia Julian is here to see you."

Ah, shit. I expected she'd hand over whatever she found when I saw her later on the balcony.

Anton glanced up. "That's the kid that was here yesterday?"

I was surprised he remembered.

"Yeah. I told her she could collect the traps I set last night," I lied. I'd have to tell her not to come around during business hours.

I hurried to the lobby. Mia smiled broadly when she saw me. "I got a good one! A big one! You're really gonna like it!" She held the trap out.

Thoughts of berating her for disturbing me vanished. "Jesus, Mia!" The hissing, snapping creature inside resembled a small lobster more than a scorpion and was like nothing I'd seen on the sample wall or anywhere else. "Where the f…" I stopped myself just in time. "Where did you find that?"

She grinned. "They're all over the place. They live in between rocks. You can't catch them with light or smells or those stupid pellets. They only eat…Pallus pilosus." She spoke the unfamiliar words slowly and carefully.

I gaped. She wasn't wearing glasses.

"Did I say that wrong? I didn't know the real name until I saw one on your bug wall yesterday."

There were over 6000 specimens on that wall. Why had that name stood out and stuck with her? "You said it right." I took the trap and gazed down at the angry, shiny black arthropod. A thin stream of yellow liquid trickled down from the spot where its back stinger struck the trap wall repeatedly. I was taken aback, not just by this amazing sample, but by Mia's ability to recognize and name its favorite prey.

She looked at me expectantly. I collected myself.

"Great work Mia, thank you!"

"I need more traps. I could have brought you a whole bunch of bugs, but I didn't want to put them all together in there."

"That would have been messy," I agreed.

"I can help. I want to be your assistant."

I was about to explain why this was impossible, then reconsidered. She probably knew more about the wildlife in this area than I ever would. Nothing prevented me from hiring more staff except lack of funds and I didn't think there was anything in the regulations about age as a requirement for employment.

"Let me think about it. I'm not sure it's allowed, but I'll check and let you know tonight back at the apartment, okay?"

"Okay!" She tapped the trap and the black tail swung around to strike the thin barrier again. "He hates the light. Bye Derek!"

She ran out the door, the gravity no burden at all to her young bones.

I returned to my lab, still a bit dazed by the fact that I might be holding a previously undiscovered specimen. Anton did a double-take when I set the shuddering trap on the work table.

"What is that?" He pushed a cascade of blonde hair back and out of his eyes. I'd never seen him this interested in anything but female mammals.

"I don't know. Scan it and tell me if it's in the database."

Anton obeyed without question, a first. He shoved the trap into the holo scanner and we both watched the lasers play across the black body. A minute later, code 807 flashed on the front screen and Anton whooped.

"Unclassified. Finally! You are in the game, man."

He went to his desk screen and pulled up a document I'd never seen before.

"What is that?"

"Claim form. You haven't needed it until now."

He checked boxes and filled in blank spaces. "What do you want to name it?"

I sat down. "I'm not sure. I have to think about that."

He pushed the form aside and opened the visiting scientist roster. "Who has what you need?"

"What do you mean?"

"What you need to get shit done. You've been here for six months and made zero progress. Who has the best venom library? We can probably trade this guy for someone's whole back catalogue."

"Dr. Martinez." I didn't have to stop and think. Alicia Martinez had been here 10 years and found dozens of new species.

"Great. I'll go talk to Dominique."

Dominique was Dr. Martinez's senior assistant. Anton grabbed the trap from the scanner and headed out.

"Hey!"

I tried to follow and he held up his hand.

"You stay here. I'll take care of this."

He did.

As I watched him negotiate with Dominique, realization washed over me. The lab assistants, all sons and daughters of Partners, were the real power here, not the Nobel-prize winning scientists they served. These weren't the bright kids–those were funneled straight into Partner track at corporate headquarters. Anton was bottom of his class at the outrageously expensive College of the Islands, a cruise ship "University" that toured Earth's equatorial seas. He'd majored in Business Communications and didn't know a trochanter from a coxa. He could barely run the mostly automated lab equipment.

I knew that Han would own the patents on anything I discovered while I worked here, but now I recalled the requirement that lab assistants be named as co-authors on any papers I wrote. Anton's success was directly tied to mine and thus far I'd done nothing to further either of our careers.

By the end of the day, I had access to the venom of 50 promising specimens from Alicia Martinez's library and she had possession of the creature. Research shouldn't be a game, but it was, and I'd just anted up.

I was so transfixed by this glut of data that I almost forgot I needed to find out if I could officially hire Mia. She could work for me secretly and bring the samples to my apartment, but I wanted to do things as by the book as I could. Breaking rules meant fines and I couldn't afford them.

As I suspected, the six corporations that owned Victoria had no child labor laws and no minimum wage. The University Annex offered a vague job title of Technician I. I entered Mia's full name and the job description as trap collection. When I showed the contract to her father that night I expected him to balk at the hundred pages of legal language. He laughed and said I'd obviously never made a restaurant reservation. I admitted I hadn't. He signed and thanked me again for humoring Mia. He didn't believe me when I said I wasn't.

Chapter Six

Mia brought in a specimen every night for the next two weeks, all of them unique and previously unclassified. If I didn't know better, I'd say she was comparing what she captured to our database and discarding anything we already had. That was impossible, though. Mia didn't have access to our database when she was out of the lab; none of us did.

These new finds created quite a stir. No one had done any serious field work within the rings in over a decade. 15 years ago the first wave of scientists, hesitant to venture too far from the safety of the lab, exhaustively catalogued the 20 kilometers around the city center. Now researchers used swarms of bots to comb the rest of the planet, 99% of which was uninhabited.

Either the first scientists hadn't done a very good job or there were long-term insect migration patterns we didn't yet understand. Regardless, after twelve straight days of "good luck," even Anton started to question my success. He cornered me and asked what kind of scam I had going.

After a moment of panic, I relaxed. He was lazy, irresponsible, and dishonest and assumed everyone else was too.

"Come out with me," I invited. "See how it works. I've got traps all over the place. I check a hundred a night. Things get really lively around 10 p.m." Which was probably when Anton was hitting his first bar.

His upper lip curled as he frowned. "No way man. You keep doing whatever you're doing and I'll keep trading the bugs for you."

Nonetheless, when Mia came in that evening with an exotic yellow and gray winged creature, I pulled her aside for a chat.

"I need some samples of what we have on the wall." I felt foolish saying this, as if she could actually pick and choose.

"You said you wanted new things."

"I did, I do, but I need to compare them to the old ones and I can't use the ones in the blocks. They aren't mine."

Mia shook her head. "Those are boring."

I spread my hands. "Research is boring sometimes. If you want to be my assistant you need to realize that. I only need one new one each week."

She reluctantly agreed to my rules and I shrugged off the nagging feeling that she actually knew which 6000 specimens were on the wall.

Anton gave me a hard time when I handed him a trap containing a bug I could have picked off the windshield of a pod, but my failures pleased him almost as much as my successes. On a normal day, I corrected him a hundred times.

My work life improved by leaps and bounds now that I'd proven my value to my coworkers. The invisible barriers I'd been slamming up against ever since I arrived at the lab began to dissolve. Supplies I needed arrived in days, not weeks. The repair technicians no longer bypassed my alcove. I was invited to join a senior scientist discussion list I didn't know existed. The nods of acknowledgement I got from the people I passed in the hall felt like bear hugs after months of being pointedly ignored.

It was all because of Mia. I worked hard to protect my asset. I instructed her not to speak to anyone but me at the lab. As far as my colleagues knew, she was merely collecting traps I'd set the night before. She wasn't allowed to come in before 6 p.m.. Anton disappeared every day at five–an hour before he was supposed to leave–so there was a good, wide buffer between the two of them.

The sight of her tromping through the lab–filthy dirty and swinging the trap like it was a school lunch box–always lifted my spirits.

They needed lifting. My research wasn't going well. Now that I had the venom I swore would be the key to success, my failures were more difficult to explain. Thankfully, no one asked. I kept Anton busy and to him, tests and experiments meant progress. Non-disclosure agreements shielded me from Della's unspoken questions. She'd spot the flaw in the equation. I had access to state-of-the-art equipment, exotic venoms, all the supplies and AI time I needed–the only variable was my intellect. I wasn't smart enough to figure this out. My graduate school success was a fluke.

Imagined conversations with Della stressed me as much as the growing list of useless venom combinations. The fear that coming home empty-handed might mean I'd lose more than my job kept me working late into the long nights.

I was so preoccupied that it was nearly seven one evening before I realized Mia hadn't come in. My stomach flip flopped. It'd finally happened. She'd been stung and was laying paralyzed on the desert floor, out of sight of the helpful drones.

Her father took too long to answer his comm. When he finally did he was puzzled by my urgency. As a parent he had access to the tracker in Mia's glasses. She was home; the apartment cams confirmed it. He hesitated a moment, then warned that she might not come in to the lab as often now that she was busy with a big school project.

His explanation rang false. Mia wouldn't skip work for one of the school projects she mocked. Not unless she was bored. Bored of catching common bugs and bored of the projects I came up for her to do in the lab after she dropped off the traps.

Shit. If the venom I needed was out there I needed Mia to bring it to me. I'd have to work harder to keep her entertained.

When, days later, she finally returned, I wasn't warned of her imminent arrival by the usual quick tap tap tap of her boots hitting the hard floor of the lab. I pulled off my glasses for a break from manipulating a complex molecule and was startled to find her standing silently beside me. She held no trap and wasn't wearing coveralls. I saw for the first time how small she was.

I couldn't resist teasing. "What happened? Drones kill all the bugs in the city?"

She slumped down at the low worktable I'd set up for her.

"No. I haven't been looking."

"I heard you've been busy with school."

She rested her chin on folded arms and gazed down at the table. "No."

I squatted down and examined her more closely. The dark circles under her eyes accentuated her woebegone expression. "You've been sick." I stated. Why hadn't Matthew told me?

She shook her head angrily. "No. I have to take the test soon."

She said this so vehemently I knew it was something out of the ordinary. "What test, Mia?"

She looked up at me with big, serious eyes. "The REA." She breathed out the vowels like a sigh.

"Oh yes. We have that on Earth too. It isn't..." I was about to say, "a big deal," when I recalled that on Victoria, it was.

M. Luke McDonell

A non-profit started the Registry of Extraordinary Abilities with good intentions–to find gifted children and give them resources to develop those gifts. Unfortunately, the corporate-funded organization quickly devolved into a pond where multinational companies speared captive fish. Though many challenged the legal right of parents to sign contracts that bound their high-scoring children to compulsory employment, the fact remained that REA was rescuing kids from poverty. 80% of children on Earth were part of the "subsistence" class and none of them could hope to climb out of that without a good education. Once a contract was signed, their lives improved immediately. In addition to a full scholarship to the best private schools, they received a stipend, good food, health care, and tutelage by experts. It was the fast track to success. Yes, they were committed to working for a certain corporation or government, but there were boundless opportunities within these huge organizations, and compulsory employment ended at age 60. Plus, no child was forced to take the exams. If a parent didn't want to bring their child to a REA center, they didn't.

On Victoria the tests were mandatory and those given after age 10 were intense. The children were treated like suspected criminals–wired up to machines that evaluated response time, eye movements, heart rate, skin temperature, and more. We didn't have to do that on Earth; kids wanted to do well. Here, apparently, some wanted to fail. High-scoring children were taken from their parents and shipped off to Earth for specialized training. Training–not education. The corporations wouldn't waste money teaching history to a math prodigy. Worst of all, the employment contracts were for life, not until retirement. No sane parent would wish that fate for their child.

Unsurprisingly, most people who came to Victoria on a 10-year contract chose not to reproduce during that period. Della and I already decided we wouldn't have Jeremy take the REA tests. If either of us became a tenured professor, Jeremy would have guaranteed admission to the University.

"The test will be different this year," I said.

She nodded. "My mom says I won't be able to choose my score."

My eyebrows shot up, but Mia didn't notice. She was tracing the fake wood grain of the tabletop with one finger.

"What kind of score do you like to get?" I asked.

"Not perfect."

Though Mia was exaggerating, I understood the problem. The tests were reactive, quickly assessing a student's strengths and weaknesses, then probing deeper into areas where they showed talent. If Mia was good at something, the test would discover this. Unless she lied–which she couldn't do this year.

"My mom says men will take me away and I won't see her or my dad for years and years." Her eyes glistened, but she didn't cry. "I don't want to go to Earth, Derek. I don't know anyone there."

We stared at each other, Mia waiting for the comfort adults were supposed to provide and me wanting to tell her not to worry. I couldn't.

"I'm going to read more about the test, Mia. Maybe I can come up with some ideas to help you not score too high. What subjects are you best at?"

She shook her head violently. "I can't tell you. If I do you won't want to be friends with me."

I took a moment to process this. "What? No. Of course I will." Mia's parents meant to protect her, but it was dangerous to give a rule like this to a young child. They'd convinced her that something she was good at would drive people away. As the father of a child fascinated by sharp objects, I understood how difficult it was to keep him safe while not discouraging him from a future career as a surgeon, but I had a new explanation for Mia's solitary afternoons on the balcony and it made me angry.

"I promise I'd still be your friend, but let's not talk about this now. Can you help me clean and reset the traps?" I knew how to comfort my son when he bumped his head, but I wasn't sure what to say to a distressed nine-year-old girl. When in doubt, try distraction.

"Sure!" She loved this task.

She grabbed a trap, placed it inside the first-stage decontamination chamber, painstakingly typed in the activation code and thumbed the scanner.

What were Mia's parents at such pains to hide? I'd known her for months and hadn't seen any evidence of genius. She had an excellent vocabulary, but kids today had access to unlimited media, so that wasn't unusual. Did she play a musical instrument? She never talked about it. I doubted she was a math or science prodigy; she regarded my screens full of data with blank indifference.

I sat down at my desk screen to begin a thorough search on 10th year REA testing procedures on Victoria when realization rolled over me like a hot, Western Sea wave. I knew what Mia was good at.

Each of the machines in the lab had a 128-character activation code. It was possible to enter this manually, but normally our glasses sent the code and we thumbed for verification. Mia wasn't wearing glasses.

"Hey Mia?"

"Yeah?" She watched the blue lasers sweep the clear walls of the trap.

"What's the serial number of that one you're cleaning?"

I wondered if she'd fall for this pathetic trick. There was no way to access the trap's screen while it was in the chamber and all the traps looked alike–to me anyway.

They wouldn't look alike to someone with a photographic memory.

She leaned close and her face glowed cerulean. "C1668079B."

"What did you catch in that one?"

"You haven't named it yet. It was that brown, fuzzy one with yellow bands on the tail."

I swiveled my screen to show her the image. "This one?"

"Yeah."

Pushing my luck, I continued. "You didn't enter the lat long coordinates where you found it." I'd just cleared them.

She jumped up, her small mouth pursed in a frown. "I did! You messed it up. You always make mistakes."

She typed coordinates into the empty section. They were correct.

I kept my expression neutral. "It's good I hired you then, isn't it?"

"Very good. I'm better than Anton, right?"

I smiled. "Much, much better. You are my best assistant."

She went up on tiptoes and hugged herself. "I never get to be the best at school."

"Hey, what do I pay you for? Cleaning traps or talking? Get back to work."

She giggled and got another trap from the box. I stared into my screen. Why hadn't I noticed this sooner? Oh, I'd noticed, and willfully ignored all the evidence because it wasn't possible. I sifted through my own fuzzy recollections and admitted that Mia had been doing the improbable for months.

Still, I didn't want to jump to conclusions. I read up on different types of memory, then spent the next few evenings exploring the length and breadth of Mia's. I had her fill out forms about the bugs she'd caught. Number of wings, legs, eyes–no matter how complicated the question, she never bothered to reference the holo scans on file. I gave her images of insects asked her to name them. She did, without consulting the database. She described where she'd caught the bugs, vacant-eyed as she pointed out features I couldn't see. Three boulders, a dead bush, black and white pebbles that didn't look like any of the other rocks. A quick search on my glasses proved her claims.

I suddenly understood what the Julians were trying to keep hidden–not a bright girl who'd score high enough on the REA exam to get shipped off-planet for training–but a valuable tool that could be used immediately.

Ten years ago her gift would have been nothing more than a conversation starter at a cocktail party. Anyone with a holo cam or iris implants could have a perfect "photographic" record of every moment of their lives.

Everything changed when corporations asserted their ownership of the audible and visible environments on their properties. "No unauthorized data collection allowed on the premises" went from fine print everyone ignored to a law that led to the banning of permanent non-medical implants and mandatory glasses settings that wiped data cached between check in and check out. Here at the lab, as in most workplaces, security was even tighter. Employees left all personal electronics at the front desk, then walked through a series of scanners and field generators that would zap any device they might try to smuggle in or out.

Corporations publicly celebrated the huge decline in intellectual property theft, and privately panicked when their own spies came home empty-handed. A quiet, intense struggle began. I sensed it happening here as well. The legions of drones, the tenseness on the faces of the guards at headquarters and the fact that I was wiped every day all demonstrated that strong forces were at work, pressing and probing, trying to find a weakness.

Soon, Han would have a new weapon: Mia.

I typed a query. As I feared, Han sector had its own REA franchise. The only reason Mia had made it this long without being discovered was that doctors and psychiatrists worlds-wide agreed that intrusive testing methods used on young children "substantially interfered" with obtaining accurate results. By age 10, children were accustomed to the yearly tests, intellectually capable of understanding why they were being monitored, and used to playing games that required physical restraints.

Mia's test scores would never be made public. Han would take her. What would happen if they used her as I suspected and she saw something truly secret, something too valuable to be left in a little girl's head? Last year, TechNational was caught offering a 100 million Victoria Monetary Unit bribe to an engineer for the battery plans used in burst drive spacecraft engines. Abstract notions of Mia being used as a spy solidified into actual dollar and credit values too large for me to comprehend.

I had to help her and there was little time. The test was in two months. She needed to be dumbed down for her exam and neither she nor the drug-testing, eye-movement tracking sensors could be the wiser.

Many of Victoria's recreational drugs would have helped Mia do badly on the test, but the REA screeners would recognize all their signatures.

I spent the next weeks in a haze of concentration. Developing a short-acting recreational-class drug with no side effects normally took years. Fortunately, I had some advantages–no administrative oversight and a library of what I'd previously considered useless neurotoxic venoms. A light dose of these could slow synaptic responses with no permanent damage. I had to find one that would make it difficult for Mia to access her memories yet show up in the blood test as no more than an insect bite.

My increased workload and the time difference made casual chats with Della next to impossible. Jeremy was misbehaving at school and Della claimed it was because he was "confused" about my absence. She allowed me to call home once a week at a specified Earth time. I couldn't appear when I wasn't expected. She promised we'd have adult time when Jeremy was asleep, but the few hours we were both at home and awake aligned once every 10 days at best.

I didn't want this arrangement to continue long-term, but for now, I was thankful for the break. My success at synthesizing promising drugs for Mia led to an unfortunate next step; I had to test them on myself. Models gave a fairly accurate account of the effect the compounds would have on the human body but couldn't predict how they would make a person feel. Lightheadedness could be the effervescent giddiness of champagne or the frightening whiteness of a near-faint. Heaviness of limb could be the pleasant lethargy induced by a hot bath or the sluggish unresponsiveness resulting from anesthesia. Increased heart rate could feel like excitement, nervousness, or panic.

With much trepidation, I swallowed a first experimental dose at the lab and rushed back to my apartment before it could kick in. Half an hour later, I was vomiting into my kitchen sink, not wanting the smart toilet to collect any data on the bizarre concoction spewing from my body.

The effects of the drugs I created ranged from none to wildly hallucinogenic. I kept tweaking, altering dosage, combining different compounds. When I had something that didn't make me sick or cause the furniture in my apartment to dance or the walls to melt, I took a memory test, aiming for a 20% reduction in my usual score.

The hours of extra work and drug testing took its toll on me. I was often too sick or sluggish to make it to work on time.

Today was no exception. I stumbled into the lab just before noon, my glasses set to near black. Anton spun slowly in his chair to face me, head tilted at a 45-degree angle, long, blonde bangs falling away to reveal one blankly blue eye. He resembled–in more ways than one–a mannequin in a store window.

"You finally discovered The Pharmacy, didn't you?" he asked.

The Pharmacy was the biggest recreational drug store in the Han sector and accounted for at least ten percent of the corporation's revenue. I kept my glasses on and didn't reply.

He frowned. I'd never seen him look stern and the expression didn't sit well on his pretty face.

"You gotta cut down. It's affecting our work."

"Our work?"

"Yes, our work. You think I brought you here so you could lie around tripping on Blue Moons? I don't understand what you do, but I know that when you aren't asking me to run 10-67 tissue tests, you aren't finding a drug to cure cancer."

It took me a moment to process this. "What do you mean, you brought me here?"

He laughed. "What, you thought there was some committee going over all the grant applications and picking the ones that would most benefit humanity?" He waved his hand around the lab. "This is a casino. One of you hits the jackpot and one of us lab assistants never has to work again. Your venom curing cancer idea is a long shot, but if you figure it out, I'm a billionaire."

"You picked me?"

He shrugged. "You made it through the initial screening process. My mom gave me 50 applicants to choose from."

"What about John Lee?"

Many of my coworkers at the University of Texas applied for the grant I got, but John was expected to win. He was the top scientist in the department and his work held great promise. When my name was called he shrugged, sighed, and went back to work.

Anton's single eye looked at me blankly. I wanted to grab a laser cutter from the bench and remove the silky yellow curtain that shielded him from the real world.

"John Lee. His name must have been on the list. You'd probably be a billionaire now if you chose him."

Anton spun lazily back to the screen and typed in the name. When the application form appeared, he laughed. "Seriously Derek? You think I want to look at that every day?" He gestured to the photo of John.

My colleague was overweight and his head turned to neck with no transition. Acne scars covered his face. I remembered thinking it odd that a full exterior body scan was required for the grant application.

I caught a glimpse of my reflection in a glass partition and saw myself for a moment as a stranger. I had the same visible cheekbones, defined chin, full head of hair, and smooth, unlined face as…as everyone else in the lab. I'd been picked because I was better looking.

I was too stunned to react when Anton pulled my glasses from my face. He stared at my eyes as if they were maps to an unfamiliar location. After puzzling for a moment, he smiled knowingly.

"Downers, huh? Take this."

He pulled a rechargeable hypo from his pocket and dangled it in front of me. "Spark. It cleans you out and wakes you up. Legal for use at the office."

I grasped the silver foil packet with clumsy fingers. I was lucky he'd decided that legal drugs were the reason for my poor health and drop in productivity.

"Thanks," I muttered, and put the hypo in my pocket.

"Seriously, Derek, back to work."

I hoped to create a drug to cure cancer and now I knew what the worst of the side effects would be–extreme wealth for Anton and the Han Corporation.

Chapter Seven

My progress on Mia's drug slowed after this. I had to do some real research to keep Anton occupied. Despite that, a month later I found a promising combination. The brown back tick, common here in the city, secreted a painkiller when it bit. The venom of the gray plate scorpion from the far north contained a mild neurotoxin. Not enough to kill prey, merely to confuse it long enough for the scorpion to grab it with pincers and feed on it while it was alive and captive.

Combined in the right proportions, the painkiller and venom created a sense of relaxation and mellow well-being and inhibited the user's ability to remember facts.

That's what I wrote in my notes, anyway. The reality was that the drug imparted a prolonged state of what I could only describe as a "just waking up" feeling. That moment in the morning when you first open your eyes and see a shaft of sunlight sliding down the worn wooden boards of the hallway outside the bedroom door. The smell of fresh-cut lawn drifts through the open window with the tick tick tick sound of a neighbor's sprinkler. A bird trills. The simple cotton sheets on the bed feel like silk, smooth and warm and luxurious, the perfect contrast to the cool dawn air that flirts with your exposed face and neck. For those few blissful moments there are no worries, no cares, no thoughts of the endless to do list. You merely exist, content in the quiet joy of a new day.

To say I liked it was an understatement.

When I took tests while on this compound, answers to familiar questions were suspended in a thick, warm liquid and I had to struggle to extract them. This didn't worry me; my anxieties were as distant as the facts and figures.

The main physical side effects included loss of appetite and a symmetrical rash on my neck and forearms that lasted about 12 hours. Psychological side effects would differ for each user. In my case, as the drug receded, the troubles in my life resurfaced one by one like the broken, barnacle-covered posts of an old pier at low tide. I lay flat on the dusty cement of my balcony thinking, another one? It took a few stiff drinks to put the genies back in the bottle.

Finally, the real test. I took a dose and went immediately to Han Headquarters. Recreational drug use during non-work hours was not only tolerated but encouraged, as the profits from these products were significant. Use at Headquarters, however, was strictly forbidden and the main security checkpoints employed the most up-to-date scanners. The REA equipment would not be more sensitive than these. I laid my hand on the glass. The doors to what was nicknamed "the wind tunnel" opened. I stepped in and forced myself to breathe normally as lasers played over my body and warm puffs of air ruffled my hair. After a few interminable seconds of delay, the far doors slid apart as usual. I'd done it! My drug was undetectable.

I grinned as I exited the monolith. It had been years since any of my work yielded the results I wanted, and it felt good to deceive the supposedly infallible systems of my employer.

Once my head cleared, or more accurately, filled back up, I realized I hadn't planned beyond this point. I'd have to tell Mia's father what I'd done and convince him to give the drug to his daughter. He may not have reached the same grim conclusions as I–

that she wouldn't be sent away to school, she'd be used as a tool immediately. He'd think I was paranoid and overstepping my bounds.

No, he and his wife had trained Mia to hide her gift for a reason and there was only one way to keep it hidden now.

I stopped mulling and called Matthew.

"Derek?" Matthew stood in a brightly-lit construction zone, framed by the stark skeleton of a building that grew as I watched.

"Yes. Can you stop by my apartment tonight? I need to talk to you about Mia. In person."

"Is she okay? Did something happen at the lab?" His hand twirled, presumably bringing up his home cams.

"Nothing happened, she's fine."

"What's this about then?" He glanced down at a screen he held, transitioning from worried father to busy foreman.

I'd hoped that, like a child called to the principal's office, he'd deduce the subject of the impending conversation by my grave tone, but he was too distracted to notice.

"Just come by. Please," I said.

He beckoned to someone I couldn't see. "Sure. I'll be out of here in an hour or so. I'm sorry we haven't had you over for dinner yet. I get sidetracked. These buildings don't build themselves!" He laughed. "Well, they do, but I've got to keep an eye on them. See you in a while." He disconnected.

When he knocked on my door, I was ready–curtains drawn against the prying eyes of the drones, a talk show playing loudly to prevent the vibrations of our voices being read on the windows, and a beer in hand.

Matthew entered, his face covered in dirt and a smile. He looked so much like Mia. Large, wide-set almond-shaped eyes, dimpled cheeks, a sharp chin set in a square jaw–his hidden in stubble.

He took the beer with a nod. "Thanks."

I gestured to the orange couch.

"You don't mind?" he asked. "I'm filthy."

"Don't worry. I found that in the recycling room and I'm putting it back there when I leave."

He flopped down, a cloud of dust rising around him, and drained half the bottle in a few gulps. When he started talking about the challenges of filling in a mostly developed city block, I realized that he'd taken my out-of-the-blue call as an awkwardly delivered social overture.

I waited until he finished his story, then pulled my rickety metal chair closer. "We need to talk."

He set the empty bottle on the floor and leaned forward, attentive but not alarmed.

"I know about Mia's memory," I said.

He stared, processing my words, remaining as still as a paused frame in a holo playback. Then he shifted and his eyes focused beyond me, as if he was watching something drift out to sea.

"Don't worry. I just want to help. Mia is," I went on despite embarrassment, "my friend. You understand?"

Matthew, still half looking at something I couldn't see, nodded. "I do. She loves spending time at your lab."

I gave him another beer and a few minutes to collect himself. "How many people know?" I couldn't have been the first person to figure this out.

He searched for the answer on the fine print of the label before finally meeting my gaze. "Just Annette and I."

I must have looked cartoon-character astonished because despite his discomfort, he smiled.

"It's true. We've been strict. Maybe too strict. The rules have been hard on her. I know she's lonely. Annette didn't want her working for you but I disagreed. Mia needs to learn how to behave around other adults. She can't stay locked in the apartment forever. She's been much happier these past few months. I hoped you wouldn't notice but I knew this day would come sooner or later." He gave me a probing glance. "Can we come to an understanding about this?" He glanced around my sparsely furnished apartment. "We've got interplanetary transport vouchers we'll never use, or, if you want plain old credits, we've got a savings account."

My confusion turned to anger. "You think I'm blackmailing you?"

Matthew held up his hands in a placating gesture. "I'm sorry Derek. I don't know anything about you. The night you came over to invite Mia to the open house you mentioned that you couldn't afford a fast ship back to Earth to visit your son. I'm sure you miss him."

I took a deep breath and stilled my temper. Many people would exploit someone in his position. He didn't know I'd spent six weeks of my precious 24 months developing a drug that might keep his daughter from corporate slavery.

"This isn't about me. It's about the REA test. Mia's worried."

Matthew's grip on the beer bottle tightened. "I am too. What do you know about REA testing?"

"I know that Mia won't be able to hide her memory this time, but I don't think she'll be sent to Earth for schooling when the officials at Han find out what she can do."

"She will. That's what happens. There've only been a handful of kids registered and all of them are gone. We'll lose her."

He gazed out the window, perhaps at a planet so distant it wasn't visible in this night sky.

"It might be worse than that." I shared my suspicion that her score would never be reported and she wouldn't be taken away to be educated. She'd be put to work immediately in corporate espionage.

I'd done more research and what I learned frightened me. Even fragments of information about technology in development fetched millions of credits.

Matthew paled as I reeled off facts and figures.

"Education won't improve her, in fact, the less she understands about what she sees the better," I said.

He stood and his face bore an extreme version of the panicked look I'd seen on students who realized they hadn't studied the right material for the final exam.

"Wait!" I grabbed his arm as he moved towards the door. "I can help. I've been working on something." I pulled a small bag from my pocket and held it out to him. Inside were four pills, two large, two small. I hoped he wouldn't think to ask how I got them out of the lab. He took the bag reluctantly and held the pills up to the light.

"Neural inhibitors. They'll keep Mia from doing too well on the test and they won't be tagged as a drug by the scanners. I've tested them." I let this sink in for a moment. "The big ones are for you. I wouldn't expect you to give anything to Mia without knowing the effects."

Matthew stared at me, brow furrowed, still processing. "What is it that you do again, exactly?"

"I work with arthropod venoms. Many of them have sedative properties. It is not unusual for residents of New Canberra to have traces of these in their blood." I gave him a significant look. "Try one. Go to headquarters. You'll make it through security. Don't try to operate heavy machinery, though. You might not remember how."

The confusion lifted from his eyes like rising fog. "I forgot…you're a doctor…"

I lowered my glasses and searched through files until I found my C.V. "Read that." I sent the file to him.

He settled his dusty goggles over his eyes and read, his hand rising occasionally to dig deeper into a link.

It was true that many of my colleagues at UT were smarter than me and their research progressed more quickly, but I was comparing myself to the best of the best. To an outsider, the difference between an A- and an A+ was irrelevant.

After ten minutes or so, Matthew took off his goggles and stared at me as if I'd appeared out of thin air. "You really can help, can't you? I had no idea. I thought you were a glorified intern. We get a lot of those here, and it's easy to buy a medical degree…"

"Not from UCSF."

He smiled ruefully. "No, not from UCSF. I'm sorry, Dr. Singh."

"Derek," I corrected.

Matthew shook the bag with the pills. "Are these safe?"

I shrugged. "Safe enough. I have no idea what would happen if someone used it every day, but once or twice, it's no worse than an insect bite."

Matthew stood. "I'll try one tomorrow. Can we meet tomorrow night on the balcony? 10 p.m.?"

"Sure."

"Thank you."

We shook hands and Matthew left. I knew very little about him, but I knew the only thing that mattered. He'd do anything to protect his daughter.

Chapter Eight

A month later, I stared blindly at a screen full of data, as
ignorant as Anton as to what I was seeing. Today was the REA test.
Matthew had tried my drug twice and found it to be as I promised.
His recall was impaired, but not in a way that was noticeable to casual
observers and he'd gotten by the drug screener at work. He, too,
found the relief from the pressure of everyday stress to be "very
pleasant." He followed that statement with a querying look. I nodded
and without speaking more about it, we both acknowledged that we'd
like to experience that more often, but wouldn't.

Would the drug work on Mia? Her memory was many times
more powerful than ours, but I couldn't risk too high of a dosage.

Matthew took Mia for a massage early that morning. I'd
urged him to do something that was not part of her normal routine
before he gave her the drug and tell her she might feel "funny"
afterwards. I didn't want her to panic. A massage was perfect.
Children didn't normally get them and the relaxed feeling was similar
to that the drug imparted.

Annette didn't know anything about our plan. Matthew knew
she'd be furious when she found out, but whoever accompanied Mia
to the testing center needed to be ignorant. Parents weren't normally
questioned, but this was an important year and the REA people

weren't stupid. A casual conversation might be monitored and analyzed.

A familiar sound startled me from my reverie–the fast, light slaps of Mia's desert boots. I turned as she flew through the door. Anton looked up from his work. He knew she collected traps for me but Mia never came in when he was here.

"Hi Derek!" she exclaimed excitedly. "I took my test and I didn't do that good." Her high spirits were at apparent odds with the content of her statement. She danced around the room, twirling and giggling.

Matthew followed her in. "Sorry to interrupt Derek. Mia wanted to stop by." His smile was broad and grateful.

Anton stared fixedly at Mia. I hurried her and her father out of the lab and into the lobby.

Mia pulled at the sleeve of my lab coat. I saw the fading rash on her arms. "My dad took me to get a massage and that made me relax." She pantomimed a waterfall with her fingers, obviously mimicking something the therapist had done. "When I relaxed, that made the test harder. I didn't know all the answers."

Matthew nodded in agreement and showed me a screen with Mia's test results: 95%. Perfect. Or more precisely, perfectly imperfect.

I squatted down so she and I were face to face. "I'm glad to hear that Mia. Let's talk about this later, okay? I'm happy you came by, but I have to work."

She threw her arms around my neck. "You are my favorite scientist."

"Oh, hey, Mia, stop that!" Embarrassed, I disentangled myself and stood.

Matthew laughed and took my hand in his strong grip. "Anything you need, anytime, just let me know. I owe you."

"Don't worry Matthew, it was my pleasure." I meant it.

"Come on Mia, we have to get to the zoo before it closes." He gave me a clap on the shoulder and they departed.

I was half tempted to join them. The realization that I'd succeeded was hitting me and I couldn't keep still. I walked back and forth along the long sample wall. The planet's mass couldn't keep the bounce from my step today. I'd done it. I saved her.

I ducked into an empty conference room to call Della. I was in luck–it was 5p.m. in Austin. I'd been distracted the last few times we spoke and I wanted to let her know I'd be more attentive now that I wasn't working late. I'd commit to calling every evening at the same Earth time, even if it meant getting up in the middle of the night or stepping out of a meeting.

She was in the backseat of a car, Jeremy next to her, and beside him a woman I didn't know.

"Hey there!" I beamed.

"Is that daddy?" Jeremy asked. He was in a blue and white striped shirt, his face covered in either mud or chocolate. A new, short haircut made him look less a baby and more a little boy. Odd–it was Della that insisted we keep his hair long even when strangers praised our "beautiful daughter." What changed her mind?

Della reached forward and wrenched the camera display to the left, shifting my view to flashes of green trees and modest one-story houses.

"I told you," her voice was the hiss of a dangerous, unseen creature, "not to call at unscheduled times. We are just getting used to you being gone."

The foliage didn't react to my shock. "I don't want you to get used to me being gone. I never wanted to be gone!"

"We both have to make sacrifices for our family. Don't call again until next week." She cut the connection.

The Perfect Specimen

I stared at the empty place on the conference room wall and began to gnaw at my thumbnail, a nasty habit I hadn't indulged in since grad school. Making a sacrifice for my family was fine if I could be sure I'd still have one when I got back to Earth.

Chapter Nine

Unwilling to face night after night in my apartment with nothing but the stars for company, I threw myself into another side project.

Once I finished my "real" work each day, I began trying to synthesize the painkiller from the brown back tick and the venom of the gray plate scorpion–the key ingredients in Mia's drug. The brown back ticks were easy to find and breed in captivity, but the scorpion was a resident of the deep south, rare and completely out of reach of Mia's considerable trapping skills. I wanted to make enough pills to get Mia through the next few years, but my current venom supply was nearly exhausted.

I'd minored in organic chemistry and enjoyed what others considered the very tedious process of synthesizing complex organic molecules from more readily available ingredients. The thrill of creating never got old, even when played out in slow motion, even when I hit a dead end and had to start over.

Mia resumed her assistant duties, appearing every evening with an insect prize. She was back to her old self now that the test was over. Still, my unfounded worry that she hadn't come in because she was bored stuck with me, especially now that I knew about her memory. I'd been shirking my duty by having her do menial labor instead of educating her. Granted, teaching her the basics of organic chemistry was throwing her into the deep end, but I was enthused about my after-hours project and she liked the idea that the molecules were puzzle pieces we needed to rearrange so they'd fit together.

Reproducing the brown back tick's anesthetic wasn't much of a challenge but the scorpion's venom was extremely complex. Weeks later, when I–or we–succeeded in the synthesis, I hoped Mia might actually understand what we'd done. It was hard to know. She used her photographic memory as a crutch, manipulating the model molecules like a holo playback. Worried that her so-called gift might actually inhibit her ability to think creatively, I tried to give her problems she couldn't solve by pulling a fact from the ocean of them that sloshed in her head. She could be a great scientist one day if she learned to take the step from certainty to speculation.

Buoyed by the success of synthesizing the compounds, I returned to my research with renewed vigor. No more fooling around. I had hundreds of venoms I needed to test against the hundreds of varieties of tumors. I couldn't fail. My career and my personal life were both at stake.

At the end of one very late night, I wearily removed my glasses, then nearly jumped when I saw Anton leaning against the doorway watching me, a stim cig in his mouth. How long had he been there?

"You done?" he asked.

"Yes," I answered tentatively. I glanced at the wall. It was nearly 2 a.m.

He jerked a thumb to the door. "Let's get a drink."

We never spent time together outside of work. "Not tonight," I protested. "Thanks for the offer, but I'm too tired. I can barely see." This was true. I'd been in hypercolor 3D space for hours and I had a hard time focusing on the desaturated world around me.

"I insist, boss."

Whatever this was about it wasn't good. Nonetheless, I was stuck with him for the next year and couldn't very well reject his first social invitation.

We took a pod to a garish residential high-rise on Ring One. The architect's influences were easy to guess–ancient Egyptian obelisks and late 20th century casinos. The gold-painted façade was brightly-lit and covered in hieroglyphics. Anton led me away from the main entrance to a small walkway that ran down the side of the building. I ran my hand across winged beetles and masked gods. This wasn't paint. The building was gilded.

Anton stopped abruptly and turned towards the wall. A laser bloomed from the center of starkly-carved lily. The beam found his face and flicked up and down like the fast-beating wings of a humming bird. Moments later, the solidity in front of us dissolved to reveal an elevator. One with no buttons, I noted when we were ensconced.

We flew upwards. Anton smirked when I involuntarily reached to the beaten-bronze wall to steady myself.

The doors opened onto a scene of overblown opulence. Everything in the huge room was white: walls, ceiling, couches, chairs, tables, and the uniforms of the waiters. Scores of low-hanging crystal chandeliers cast a deep blue vibrating light that stressed my tired eyes. Based on the well-dressed crowd and the drinks and drugs being served, this was one of the exclusive private clubs I'd heard about.

Anton greeted the doorman with a handshake and a slap on the shoulder. A short discussion ensued. I gathered–from the way the doorman flapped his hands at me like he was shooing a fly–that I wasn't properly dressed. My work uniform had never looked so shabby. My t-shirt, normally covered by my lab coat, evidenced strange, Rorschach-like splotches in the ultra-violet light. Anton palmed a screen the doorman held out and moments later a thin, young man offered me a long silver coat. I took it, amused that clothing so garish served as camouflage here. Indeed, my sole function now was to reflect the glory around me.

The two beefy security guards let us pass.

As Anton sauntered towards a booth in the back, I realized I'd never seen him fully in his element. At the lab, IQ points trumped credits and his arrogance was subdued. Here, heads turned as he passed. Willowy girls with hair like sparkling waterfalls bent towards him for kisses and men in suits worth more than my grant gave him rough hugs.

Once we were seated, he evaluated me and appeared satisfied with my tourist's awe of my surroundings.

"You been here before?" he asked unnecessarily.

He flagged down a waiter and ordered a bottle of CZ, an expensive Earth vodka. This was getting stranger and stranger. I tried to imagine what prompted this. I had no answer, other than that Anton meant for me to feel stupid and out of place. Perhaps as payback for how he felt at work?

The vodka arrived with a bucket of ice and two small glasses. Anton poured, handed me a drink, then held his up for a toast. I clinked uncertainly.

He smiled broadly. "To you, for getting me out of the shithole of a job my mother forced on me."

He pressed a button on the table and a translucent white dome formed over us. I viewed the rest of club as through a steamy glass shower door. Faint hissing replaced the loud atonal music and the buzz of the crowd.

Anton snapped his fingers to get my attention, then, with all the theatricality of a children's party magician, pulled back the sleeve of his long shirt. As obvious as stars in a midnight sky, I saw the same symmetrical rash I'd had on my own arms.

He flipped his hand to face me as if for a high five. I didn't move.

He shrugged and knocked back the vodka in one gulp. "I totally misjudged you. I shoulda known." He made air quotes with his fingers. "The quiet ones. Doing research that no one else understands. Perfect. Lots of time to sneak in other projects."

A group of three women strayed near to our table, their nearly transparent dresses hiding little of their sculpted bodies, but Anton kept his eyes on me.

"This is great shit! It's smooth and un-fucking-detectable. You know how many of my friends have been trying to find ways to get high at work? You are a genius, man. I'll sell it 'unofficially' for a couple years, then take the formula to R&D and make a fortune on the patent." He tapped his glass on the table for emphasis. "My patent."

I was still too stunned to speak.

He had no problem filling the silence. "I didn't put two and two together until that kid came in a few weeks ago. It was obvious you were hung over nearly every day and I saw your weird rash a few times, but I figured you were allergic to some plant out in the undeveloped lots. Then she came in, all spacey, with the same rash." He shook his head in mock approbation. "I never thought you'd be the type to test a drug on a little girl. I'm…" His fake frown flipped up to a grin, "really fucking impressed man. That was brilliant. She wouldn't know what was going on and you could test the dosage and effects on a different body weight. Sure, it's amoral, and illegal if you subscribe to the AGE human rights doctrine, but Victoria doesn't. Good call doing your work here."

He refilled his glass and held it up for a toast again. When I didn't respond he laughed and drank alone.

There was no point in denying what I'd done. "How did you make the pill?" I asked.

He relaxed back into the white leather booth, completely at ease. "My mom is a Partner. I told her I needed access to all your data. I didn't understand the formulas, but I saw you'd been outputting pills. This last one," he patted his hip pocket, "you made 20 times so I figured you got it right. If it was something to get rid of tumors it would have been in your usual folders, not hidden away like it was. Anyway, the printer said it was only mildly toxic so I made one and tried it."

I couldn't believe someone would print a mystery drug and ingest it. Anton was more and less of an idiot than I'd ever imagined. "You shouldn't have been in my files. I developed that as an exercise. Playing around helps me clear my head. You could have poisoned yourself." I tried to speak authoritatively, as the boss I'd been, but Anton was in control and he knew it.

"No, it wasn't just an exercise. It's almost impossible to get a drug past Headquarter's security and certainly not one that makes people feel so good."

He rubbed his pectoral muscles in a way that made me uncomfortable.

"You designed this specifically for Headquarters employees— the people with the most credits and power on this planet."

Anton had no idea of my real motivation. I didn't care if he stole my formula, I cared that once he took it to Han's R&D department, Mia would no longer be able to use it to escape REA. She had one or two more years at best. Perhaps by then her parents could figure out another way to shield her. There was no arguing with Anton if he had access to my private files. I did the shot of vodka I held and sank back into the cushions.

"Fine, you can have it. Believe what you want, but I was only fooling around. I do side projects to jumpstart my creativity. I am here to find a way to knock out tumors, that's the fact. Check my files since you can access them all. I've made a lot of progress in the last few weeks." I was an unconvincing liar.

Anton stretched, then leaned forward, resting both arms lazily on the table. "You aren't going to work on that stuff anymore."

"What?"

His pupils were huge. He'd taken a larger dose of the drug than I ever had.

"You work for me now. We have to figure out how to get rid of the rash. I want no side effects or someone is going to catch on."

I raised my hands to stave off his greed. "No way. I'm done. You can experiment with it. I have other things to do."

Anton's laugh was muted by the privacy shield that surrounded us. "No, you don't. Maybe you haven't noticed, but you're no good at finding cures for cancer."

He'd aimed low and the blow stuck hard.

"Give it up. Move on. You've got a talent for recreational drugs," he said.

I shook my head. "No, I was lucky."

"I'll share the profits with you. I think an 80/20 split is more than fair. Here's an advance on our first month's sales. Use it to get some furniture."

How did he know I didn't have furniture? He flung a credits card onto the table and my retort died before I uttered it. The sum of 100,000 VMUs flashed repeatedly on the small screen. Victoria Monetary Units. Hard currency. I did a quick conversion in my head and realized this was the equivalent of six years salary at the University.

I had the same choice to make on Earth when I graduated–academia or private sector. It was easy to be idealistic back then–before I was married, before I had a child and a mortgage. Even so, my greed flared and died in only a moment. Money wasn't what I wanted.

I turned the card over and pushed it slowly back to him. "No thanks. I don't need furniture."

His concentration was fully absorbed by the glass of vodka he swirled in front of his eyes. "You want a bigger cut? Sorry dude. 20% is all you get. This is what happens next. First, you figure out how to fix the rash, second, you get to work on another drug. Otherwise, I'm sending a full report back to the University of Texas on what you've been doing with your time, as well as proof that you tested your 'exercise' on a nine-year old girl. I've got holo scans of Mia, printer records, everything. None of this is illegal on Victoria, but you'll probably lose your University job thanks to one of their uptight rules."

I got a sliding, dizzy feeling reminiscent of one of my failed drug experiments. Anton didn't know much about Earth law, or he'd realize he was delivering a much stronger threat. The legalization of a handful of recreational drugs in North America had only been allowed in conjunction with harsh penalties for selling or providing drugs to minors–harsh as in fifteen years prison for a first offense, no parole, and I was bound by these laws. Not only that, Mia would be dragged into the investigation. Someone would undoubtedly notice I'd given her the drug on the day of the REA exam and she'd be retested.

I had over a year left on my grant, but with the evidence he'd collected, Anton could keep me here indefinitely.

As if reading my mind, he reached into his bag and pulled out a large, Han-certified screen. On it was a ten-year contract, my name in a bold font across the top. This was the shortest legal document I'd seen on Victoria. My eyes flitted across the page. I'd work for Anton,

all my discoveries were the property of Han, and my base salary
would be more than double that of a tenured professor at UT.

Anton nodded encouragingly as he poured me another shot.

I drank without tasting. I was beyond panic now. Even if I
signed, Anton still held an ax over my head. If I didn't deliver the
results he wanted, he could boot me back to Earth with data that
would put me in prison.

I set the empty glass carefully on the table and stood. "I need
time to think."

"No, you don't. Palm this and get it over with," he slurred.

"Not now."

"Sit down!" He compressed the words into a sloppy two-
syllable command.

One thing was still more important to him than destroying
my life. "You really want me to stay?" I began to unbutton the
reflective silver jacket. My stained t-shirt and uniform pants appeared,
centimeter by centimeter. One of the nearly-naked women turned to
face me, curious to see how this scene played out.

Anton waved his hands as if warning a stratoshuttle not to
touch down. "Fine, go. Think. Don't take that jacket off. It's yours."

My head whirled on the elevator ride down. I'd
underestimated Anton. He wasn't smart, but he was clever. Had all
my years in school left me as bright and brittle as a light bulb, ready to
be smashed by the first hard object I encountered?

No.

I went back to my apartment and did an inventory of my
belongings. It didn't take long. I hadn't brought much, and nothing I
really cared about. I smiled ruefully at my misguided idea that
Hawaiian shirts would be proper attire in this hot alien city. They
hung unworn in the closet. I made the bed and lay on it, still in the
silver jacket, and stared out at the stars.

The Perfect Specimen

Chapter Ten

I went to work the next morning and was not surprised to find I was locked out of all my files. Anton appeared hours later, disheveled and yawning. He smiled when he saw me sitting motionless on the stool, screen in front of me blank.

"Hang on." He pulled a hypo from his pocket, pressed it to his forearm, blinked, and shook his head like a dog shaking water from its coat. "Done thinking?"

I unfolded my arms and held my palms up in surrender. "You win."

I expected a fist pump; all I got was a snort. "Yeah, I know. I won a long time ago." His bloodshot eyes were now clear and he fixed them on me with stim-fueled intensity. "I won when I was born."

What a prick. "We need to get some things in order before I sign the employment contract."

His eyebrows fell. "Like what?"

"Like file ownership. You can access my files but you aren't the creator. I'm a UT employee now and if we leave all these research files in my name, you and Han will own the patents but UT has a right to non-commercial use of the work. I'm not an expert in contract law, but the lawyers at UT are and they didn't allow me to walk away from my real job for two years without expecting a payback. You don't want the formula for the drug to leave the planet, do you? Your whole plan goes down the drain if it does."

Anton glared. "Are you bullshitting me?"

I shook my head. "I am not. Check with the other research assistants. The best scientists from Earth wouldn't be here if Han could deny them access to their own work once the contract ended."

Anton scowled, but made his way straight over to Dr. Martinez's assistant Dominique. While I waited for her to confirm what I'd told him, I cleaned traps and triple wiped the GPS data they held in their tiny brains.

Anton returned, annoyed. "You're right. We can change the file creator and owner information but it is going to be a huge pain in the ass. We both have to palm and enter security codes for every single file." He glared at the screen. "You've got a hundred thousand files in there, don't you?"

I smiled. "Don't worry, it won't be as bad as you think. As you know, my special project," I made air quotes to be sure Anton understood, "is in a hidden directory, separate from my cancer research. We'll do all those files first. It might take a few hours, but when we are done, those files will be out of the hands of UT."

"Let's do it. No fucking around though, Derek."

"You can run the process. I won't do anything but palm the screen and type in my code."

Anton unlocked the files and we began. It did take hours, but every time the green light flashed and the file name changed, one link of the chain that held me to Victoria burst and I fought to contain my rising elation. I wasn't done yet...

Anton was out of patience when we finished. I don't think he'd worked that hard in months. "That's it?"

"Not quite. It isn't practical to assign all the cancer research material to you; it would take a thousand hours. I don't want to deal with that and neither do you. On the other hand, UT doesn't have a right to all this work, as far as I'm concerned. It was done on Han equipment, with insects from Victoria. I'll have to turn some of it over to them, but the rest? Fuck 'em. Let's delete it."

Anton considered and I prayed that all the misconceptions he had about me being a conniving, greedy bastard held firm.

He smiled at the long list of legitimate research files like they were dynamite and he was a blowtorch.

"I hated running those tests." With a few quick gestures, he highlighted everything.

I jumped between him and the screen. "Hang on! We have to save some of it. I don't mind looking like I was working slowly, but they aren't going to buy the fact that I did nothing for nearly a year! UT is going to be angry enough as it is that you've hired me away. We don't want to draw attention to ourselves and you don't want to look like you offered a 10-year contract to an idiot."

"Fine, but before I let you touch any of this…" He took all the files related to the drug and moved them to his own directory, out of my reach. "Have at it, but I'm going to keep an eye on what you're doing."

"Please do." I took the seat in front of the screen. "I'm going to be deleting, that's it. You can disable all other functions if you'd like." Anton had administrator-level power and no idea how to wield it.

"Nah, I'll just watch." He put on his glasses and from the way his head twitched, I knew he was already doing something else.

I began the culling. First pass–pure vanity. I deleted any projects that were embarrassing failures. Next, I axed any work that might be of value to Han but not UT. With much trepidation, I deleted all my work on synthesizing organic compounds, which included the painkiller from the brown back tick and the venom of the gray plate scorpion. I was glad I hadn't stored this data in my secret directory or Anton would have it now.

When I brought up Mia's personnel file, Anton sat up. He wasn't as preoccupied as he'd seemed. "What are you doing?"

"Firing her. I don't want her around anymore. I can't use her again, anyway. Now that you're in charge we can get real test subjects." My finger hovered above the red X. "That okay with you?"

Anton's head lolled back to observe a different ceiling in some more interesting virtual reality. "Fine. I don't know how you put up with her. I'd rather test shit on myself than deal with some stupid kid yammering."

I pressed the button and silently said goodbye as Mia's freckled face vanished.

"All done," I said.

Anton groaned. "Great. Now sign this and go get yourself some new shoes. I can't look at those anymore." He threw the screen with the employment contract onto the work table.

"I'll sign–tonight at that club. Whatever it's called. I'll meet you by the wall at eight."

"No way. I'm not taking you there again. You'll ruin my reputation."

I smiled. "Don't worry. I'll get new shoes and wear that ridiculous jacket."

Anton held back his bangs and examined me like I was merchandise in a shop window. "Fine. One last time. Never again after this."

I agreed. "Never again."

"I'll meet you there at ten, not eight. No one gets there at eight."

"Perfect. See you then."

Chapter Eleven

Anton, of course, was late. I tried waiting by the invisible elevator doors but a security guard appeared from the shadows and shooed me away. I paced the sidewalk in front of the garish building, blisters forming where my ill-fitting new shoes rubbed my heels. I hated wasting money on these ridiculous lime green loafers, but I couldn't risk angering Anton.

Pods stopped more and more frequently as the night wore on. I'd forgotten it was Friday. At last, one of the egg-like spheres disgorged Anton. He was all in white with the exception of his glasses–a narrow slash of black across his tanned face.

I stopped walking so he wouldn't notice my limp.

He strode purposefully by without pausing. "Come on." He wanted me out of the blinding spotlights and into the obscurity of the side passage.

This time, Anton got me into the club with nothing more than a brief explanation. We were seated at the same table. His table, I wondered?

The place was much more crowded than last night and the music more uptempo. Some of the women moved back and forth rhythmically, a prelude to dancing.

"Waddaya want?" Anton yelled over the din.

I ticked off my needs on my fingers. "Painkiller. Stimulant. Alcohol. And that privacy shield."

"Anything else?"

I ignored his sarcasm. "No, that's it."

He ordered and I examined the room carefully. Two bouncers flanked the elevator. Better-dressed security staff wandered the room but their relaxed postures told me that the overdoses and lover's quarrels wouldn't happen until much later.

The waiter returned with the bottle of vodka I'd hoped Anton would request. My drugs were presented like jewels–two custom hypos on a silver tray. I grabbed them and pressed them one after another to my forearm.

"Hey, slow down," Anton advised, indicating the spent cans I'd discarded. "We've got better stuff than that."

The pain in my feet subsided and my already elevated heart rate accelerated. "Good. Let's have a drink."

The glass I held out shook.

Anton pulled the cork from the bottle and poured. "I know I said I'd never bring you here again, but I will. Next time you make a drug that can get past scanners we'll celebrate. They don't all have to be like this first one. People need different things."

I'd been too preoccupied to notice the rash on Anton's arms.

"Turn on the shield. We shouldn't be talking about this in public," I said.

Anton activated the shield and began to describe the characteristics of his favorite drugs and variations of these he'd like me to develop. I kept his vodka glass full and nursed mine, not sure whether it would be better to be drunk or sober for what was to follow.

As the night wore on, the blue lights morphed to a more intense purple and the crowd began to form clots based on drug preference. Those on depressants settled in the sunken seating area in back. Those on stimulants orbited the performance artist in front, gyrating to a beat the privacy shield obliterated. Alcohol lovers gathered around the glittering central bar where half a dozen bartenders shredded and juiced exotic Earth fruits and mixed them with whatever benign native plants they'd managed to coax into toxicity.

I needed to act now. Della wouldn't approve of my plan but I was sure she would do the same if someone threatened to keep her from her child for 10 years.

I picked up the bottle of vodka and dumped the remaining alcohol into the ice bucket. Anton didn't notice. He'd gone from envisioning the drugs we might develop to describing the pluses and minuses of those he'd taken.

Even empty, the cut crystal vessel was heavy. I brought it down hard and fast against edge of the small stone table. It shattered spectacularly, but the privacy shield kept the sight and sound of breaking glass from the security guards.

I was left with the neck–a perfect circle of jagged triangular glass shards, glittering and sharp as knives. I hesitated for a moment, then remembered Anton's boast that he'd won when he was born and my arm jabbed towards him almost of its own accord.

It was a weak thrust; the points barely broke the cloth on his shirt. Nonetheless, a dark ring slowly formed on his chest. At first no more substantial than a stain left by a wine glass on a tablecloth, blood quickly filled the circle then ran in streams down his thin white shirt. The drug must have dulled the pain. He didn't yell, just stared at me in dumb surprise.

"Sorry Anton…" I began, then everything happened at once. The club's systems finally figured out something was wrong. The privacy shield snapped off. Loud music and conversation overwhelmed our quiet void. Anton's blood was black in the suddenly blue light. Small silver drones circled me like hungry mosquitoes. Human security guards followed.

Comprehension dawned on Anton's face. Despite being drunk and drugged, he guessed my plan. He grabbed a napkin to hide his wound and jumped up, putting himself between me and the nearest guard.

"I'm fine!" he shouted above the din. "There's no problem here."

No one listened to him. Sharp, stinging pains flared on my face, chest, and arms and I saw the drones were firing tiny hypos. I managed to remove only one of the needle-sized darts before my arms stopped working and I fell sideways onto the couch, helpless and fighting panic. A beast of a guard stepped around Anton, hoisted me with one beefy arm and dragged me away from the table. The crowd parted, hardly sparing us a glance. I realized that passing out was uncouth but probably not unusual here. We headed towards the back of the club.

Anton followed, frantic. "It was an accident. My fault, not his." When the guard didn't respond, he shouted. "You don't have to do this! I'm a member!"

I wanted to smile, but couldn't. Victoria boasted of having no violent crime thanks to the "invincible" security systems. If this wasn't a private club for Partners and Executives I'd have been stunned the moment I broke the bottle. The illegal shield gave me the seconds I needed. Now, we all had a problem. I'd broken the terms of my contract and this club wouldn't want news of their security weakness to leak out.

The back office buzzed with tense energy. A wall of screens showed Anton and me from every angle, frozen at the moment I'd stuck him with the bottle. A tall man in a charcoal gray suit spoke in a low, angry voice to a group of cowed-looking men and women.

"...especially when a privacy screen is up. Victor, can you tell me why the breakage detector didn't work? The sweeper should have been over there before the glass hit the ground. Marcy, what part of 'aggressive stance' is your system not catching? Did anything not fail? Clearly..." He noticed us and slammed the door shut.

The guard brought me to what looked like a break room and dropped me onto a long narrow couch. Breathing took all my concentration. I was glad I'd taken the stimulant earlier or I'd be unconscious now and I desperately needed to know what was about to happen to me.

The man in the charcoal suit entered a moment later.

Anton turned to him and continued his urgent protests. "I told him to break the bottle! He didn't stab me. I fell into it."

The man shook his head. "I'm afraid that 36 cameras don't lie, even if you do Mr. Hale. Dr. Singh isn't a resident. Any assault by a non-resident on a resident–which never happens–requires a fine and deportation." He turned to the beefy guard. "I need a pod at the ground-level freight elevator."

The guard waved his hands in an intricate pattern, then nodded. "On its way."

Anton blanched. One hand clutched the napkin to his chest, the other fluttered a screen in front of the man's face as if trying to cool him. "You can't take him. Call my mother, Emilia Hale. You work for her!"

The man turned his full attention to Anton. "We won't be calling your mother or any other Partner. I will seal your wound and get you a new shirt. Whatever you and your boyfriend were playing at..." his eyes were hidden behind glasses but his mouth was set in an angry line, "that kind of thing doesn't happen here. Didn't happen here," he emphasized. "Keep an eye on them," he instructed the guard as he left.

Anton crouched down so that we were eye to eye. He glared. "Nice try, but you aren't getting off this planet. Once you sign this employment contract you'll be a resident and this will be nothing more than a typical Friday night."

He shoved the screen into my face as if I could sign with my nose.

"No." My lips barely moved and the screen muffled my voice.

"Get away from him," the guard instructed Anton.

Anton stood and smiled like a kid holding a magnifying glass over a bug. "I still own you, Derek. I've got the evidence I need to ruin your life."

"You don't own me," I croaked, "you own all the files related to the drug you developed. I had nothing to do with it. All I did in the last year was fail to cure cancer. Check the records."

Anton's shocked, sweaty face was the last thing I saw before the sedatives finally sent me into blackness.

Chapter Twelve

When I opened my eyes again, I was in a dim, coffin-like space. Lights flared to full brightness when I sat up, revealing a white box just over a meter wide and tall and long enough for an adult to lie down, the entire floor a mattress. My mouth was dry and I was stiff and sore. I had trouble gathering my thoughts, probably the aftereffects of the sedatives. What was this place? A spaceport cube hotel possibly, though my sluggish brain also offered the unwelcome suspicion that a jail cell in a clean, neat city like New Canberra might look a lot like this.

My unasked question was answered by distinctive rumble of a burst drive engine powering up.

Alarm cleared my head. I searched the walls and found an area that might be an interactive screen. I slapped my hand onto it and a generic welcome image appeared.

"Where am I?" I rasped.

A cheap, synthesized voice replied. "Passenger liner ARTEMIS, Level 3, cabin 346-A."

I stared at the text and promotional photos that appeared on the screen in conjunction with the spoken words. The Artemis was a class 5 transport ship. I knew what that meant—cheap and slow.

"Where are we now?"

The images swirled then split apart to form a small Earth on the left, a small Victoria on the right, and a bright, blinking dot not far from Victoria. "We are on jump 6 of 97 en route to Earth."

"You've got to be kidding."

The ship didn't respond to my statement.

I'd expected my attack on Anton would lead to a deluge of paperwork and fines–the way anything "criminal" was dealt with on Victoria–and I'd need to fake hostility, maybe even mental illness, in order to actually be deported. Never did I dream they would throw me on a ship immediately. Jump 6 meant the ship left at least a day and a half ago.

I reached forward and stabbed at the button that should open the door to this cabin, half-worried I was locked in, but the door slid aside. I peeked out and saw a walkway, other cabins across from me, and people walking unhurriedly. I re-shut the door.

The burst drive engines were almost fully powered. I'd only been on a ship like this once but the sensation was so unique it was impossible to forget. The bass rumbled in my guts, then there was silence and the feeling of being between breaths, waiting. After a moment the feeling was gone and the slow quiet drone of the engines winding up began again.

"I need to send a message to Della Mills, ID number 38462795, Austin, Texas." I'd missed our scheduled call. Though it wouldn't be the first time, was my number disconnected when she'd tried it? What if she called the lab? Would someone tell her I was no longer on Victoria? I was too groggy to consider all the options but was sure that at this moment Della was at best annoyed, and at worst, extremely worried.

"You have zero credits available for long distance communications," the sing-song voice informed me.

The planets on the screen disappeared, replaced by the Han Interstellar Bank logo. My withdrawals and deposits for the last three months were displayed. The final withdrawal–two days ago when I was unconscious–emptied my account. The generous monthly stipend, which I'd barely touched and planned to use to pay for Jeremy's first year of college, was gone.

I scrubbed my hands through my tangled hair. I'd forgotten that Han wouldn't pay transportation costs back to Earth if I breached my contract. After Anton presented me with his ultimatum, my mind had gone into overdrive and I'd considered and rejected 100 different scenarios. It was no surprise that I'd overlooked a few details.

I needed to get cleaned up and stimmed up so I could think clearly enough to compose a letter to Della. "Where is my luggage?" I asked the screen.

Too many seconds of silence followed. "You have no checked baggage. Please check the interior storage bins for any personal belongings."

Nearly invisible white panels on either side of me slid up to reveal…nothing. I patted my pockets. They were empty as well. Though I'd expected this, the panicky feeling of having forgotten to pack something important momentarily overwhelmed me. I reached for my glasses. No glasses.

"Where are the showers?" I asked.

The screen showed a green dashed line from my cabin to just around the corner.

The stark white cube seemed to breathe a sigh of relief as I slid out and stumbled onto the ridged plastic walkway. It was probably hours past its regularly scheduled cleaning. I must have looked more rumpled and disoriented than the average space traveler as the others in the corridor gave me wide berth.

The washroom was spacious and I was glad to see a shelf full of the same disposable paper jumpsuits I'd worn on the trip over. Yes, they were the mark of the low-budget traveler, people like me stuck in coffins with no room for spare clothes, but I didn't care.

I spent half an hour under the hot, not-yet-stale water, trying to wrap my head around my situation. On the plus side, I was off Victoria and out of Anton's greedy grasp. His threats to expose the "drug testing" I'd done on Mia vanished once he took ownership of my files. Also, he couldn't reveal the existence of the drug without ruining his plan to sell it illegally. The club would erase all official evidence of my assault on him to preserve their reputation. My deportation would be due to a vaguely-worded breach of contract.

On the other hand, Anton was a spoiled child and I'd dangled a new toy in front of him then thrown it far out of his reach. He'd do anything he could to ruin me. My boss at UT had probably already received a scathing review of my performance paired with some menacingly vague legal language about contractual irregularities. If Han did release any of my research files, my colleagues would see nothing but failure after failure, cancer cells thriving, tissue dying.

I shut off the water and turned on the fans. As the condensation cleared from the shower stall mirror, I saw a man with crazed hair, bloodshot eyes, and a happy smile playing on the edges of his lips. I'd done it. I'd escaped and, all evidence to the contrary, not without a prize.

As I dressed my stomach growled, reminding me I hadn't eaten in days.

The way to the lower-class lounge was indicated by insultingly frequent signage, as if two meters was longer than anyone could be expected to hold a thought. When the doors slid open at my approach, what I'd taken to be the sounds of quiet conversation thundered over me in a roar. The large room was a circus of humanity.

This was meant to be a cafeteria. The food and beverage-dispensing machines embedded in the back wall were the only source of nourishment for most of the passengers. Four-top tables, at least 100 of them, were bolted to the floor in rows. The 400 seats should have been more than enough to accommodate the thousand low-budget travelers who'd presumably be eating at different times. Unfortunately, no one wanted to spend their waking hours in the tiny one by two meter "cabins." Savvy travelers rushed to the lounge as soon as they boarded, claimed a table, and unofficially owned it for the next five weeks. The place resembled a flea market near closing time, full of the junk no one wanted to buy. Suitcases and bags surrounded each table to delineate territory. Clothing was draped on the backs of chairs to air out. Kids played games on the floor as their parents talked or worked above them.

I was a day and a half late to the party. I'd never get a seat. I didn't mind. I'd been immobile for too long. I picked my way through the maze to the free food vending machine. The plain gray metal box cowered next to the bright, animated machines that dispensed for credits. I punched in an order for 500 calories of food chips and a stim soda and took the cup and equally cardboard wafers to one of the small, porthole windows.

The random white pinpricks of light resolved into familiar constellations once the food and drink hit my bloodstream. I'd spent many nights on the lounge chair on the apartment's balcony, my glasses patiently teaching me the language of alien stars.

I felt a pang for the hot, heavy moonless nights, the ugly orange couch, my abandoned Hawaiian shirts and of course, for Mia. Part of me was glad I'd been forced off the planet. A year from now

I'd have felt even more responsible for her and leaving would have been a betrayal.

Before I met Anton at the club, I'd stopped by Matthew's building site. I needed to tell him what was about to happen so he could explain to Mia why I'd disappeared. Even so, she might be on the balcony now, hoping there'd been a mistake and that I'd return.

My guilt at abandoning her was subsumed by a more disturbing realization. While her dirty oversized coveralls, tangled hair, half a dozen freckles, and skeptical blue eyes were as familiar to me as my own face, I couldn't picture my son Jeremy in as much detail. I reached for my non-existent glasses–again. I remembered only fragments of the holo clips Della sent me. He rode a tricycle...but was it red or blue? What was he wearing at his third birthday party? Did he have the same gap between his front teeth that Mia did? I was horrified to admit I had no idea. I used to tell people that the best part of my day was when I got home from work and Jeremy threw himself into my arms, his shrill cry of "Daddy!" nearly piercing my eardrums, but now I couldn't recall what it felt like to hold him.

When I told Matthew we needed to speak privately, he led me beneath the grumbling guts of a plasticrete factory. Tiny builder bots scurried around our feet en route to collect their liquid cargo as I related the events of the day before and what I expected would happen in the next 27 hours.

Matthew sputtered out apologies, aghast that helping Mia had put my career in jeopardy and led me to consider violence. I assured him my career was not in danger. No matter what stream of digital slander Anton spewed down to Earth, my colleagues at UT would believe this simple truth: Han tried to force me to sign a 10-year contract. Bribery, blackmail, entrapment–it didn't matter how they'd gotten to me, just that I resisted and returned to work. Victoria's gravity was pulling the best and brightest minds from Earth and the universities were frantic. I suspected that from now on my department would forbid staff from applying for research grants from any of Victoria's six corporations. My job was safe.

As for the violence? I wasn't going to hurt Anton. Not much anyway. By the time he got home from the club the nu-skin would have removed any visible trace of the wound and I suspected he never wore the same shirt twice, even ones without rips and blood stains.

Matthew reluctantly agreed that there were few other escape routes open to me. As the sun set behind the skeletal outline of a building that was yet to be, I asked for a few favors. First, that he and his wife wouldn't leave Mia alone every day after school. When she was older she'd learn to hide her gift well enough to interact with her peers. Until then, she needed companionship. Second, he'd find another way for her to fail the REA tests. My drug wasn't the safest or best solution and I was pretty sure Anton–sloppy and obvious– wouldn't be able to keep it beneath the scanners for an entire year. And finally, I needed Mia's help on a project I'd continue on Earth.

Matthew listened attentively, agreed, then gave me a brief, embarrassed hug. I promised I'd contact him as soon as I could. He walked me back out to the street and waved as the pod rolled me to an uncertain future.

A dozen stim-soda fueled children thundered past, startling me out of my reverie. I held my drink and chips above the fray, glad to be back in familiar, overcrowded chaos. Austin was a city of millions and only in my small backyard could I swing my arms without hitting someone. The clean, pretty streets of New Canberra had unnerved me.

Once the storm of children had blown by, I returned my attention to the porthole and the one incongruous element. The yellow blot that was Victoria wasn't part of the starfield that I would miss.

What combination of fear and arrogance had convinced me that traveling light-years from home would solve my problems? I had to give Anton credit for one thing. He was right–I was no good at finding a cure for cancer. I'd spent the last decade making excuses. I didn't have the right equipment. I didn't have the right samples. On Victoria, everything I said I needed was given to me. My bluff was called and my flawed logic exposed. My grant-winning proposal had been nothing more than a detailed fantasy. I was looking for the perfect specimen, one with venom that would require only a gentle nudge from me to miraculously cure cancer. It was time to pack up my ego and admit I'd chosen the wrong career.

Back at UT, I loved sneaking away from the grim seriousness of our lab and visiting "the dark side," the modern 20-story building that housed the biomedical engineers. My colleagues mocked them for "curing" freckles and gray hair and creating the hypo that changed fingernail color in an instant, but to be fair, they'd also developed the sunscreen pill that made it possible to survive the intense UV radiation on Victoria. Most importantly, they generated the revenue that kept the rest of the university afloat.

My group hadn't developed a salable product in years. Though we envisioned ourselves the future saviors of humanity, everyone else saw us as an unstaunchable wound, bleeding money. As a result, we got only a fraction of a percent of the annual budget. I would no longer blame my own failures on financial constraints, but most of my coworkers could and with good reason. John Lee–the brilliant scientist who should have won the grant–could only afford an hour a week on ARIEL, the disease-modeling AI. Della needed an army of robots to collect soil samples; she had two. Grad students had to be paid, so we never had enough staff to get time-consuming projects done. We were on a slow, sure, death-spiral, drowning in good ideas we couldn't implement.

This was about to change. I was finally going to make a real contribution. Not by curing cancer, but by mainlining cash straight into our group so that my colleagues could. My drug was going to be a blockbuster and UT would own the patents on the formula.

How? I'd beat Anton to the punch. As long as he was selling pills on the black market he wouldn't and couldn't trademark the drug or the HQ scanners would be updated to sniff for it.

When he ran out of the raw materials I'd loaded into the printer he'd have a hell of time getting more. Gray plate scorpion venom was rare. He might be able to weasel a small amount from friends and colleagues, but at some point he'd realize the illegal sales were over and it was time to go legit. He'd bring his "discovery" to the attention of his mother. After she finished berating him for not telling her sooner, she'd assign a team to synthesize the compounds and patent the formula.

They'd be too late. I'd already done this work and with Anton's unwitting blessing, permanently deleted it from Han's archives. Fortunately, I had a backup copy.

The copy in Mia's head. She'd watched my numerous failures and eventual success. If Matthew did as I asked and convinced her to transcribe my work, drawings of the molecules and formulas would soon be on their way to my intern—on plastene, nothing digital—carried by courier. A few months from now the drug would be patented by the University of Texas and human trials beginning. Anton would be locked out of the Earth market.

Han would be furious but they wouldn't make any formal accusations. Firstly, there was no evidence I'd synthesized the venoms while on Victoria. Secondly, everyone knew it was virtually impossible for data to leave the University Annex. Suspicion would fall on Anton.

Perhaps we'd made a bargain. I gave him the drug to sell illegally and he found a way to get me the formula. The whole thing would be hushed up. His next job would probably be on a fishing boat. I smiled as I imagined his perfect blonde hair dulled to brittle straw by salt air and harsh wind.

A couple vacated their precarious perch on an oversized, L-shaped metal pipe and I scooted in, waving apologies to a pair of teens hovering nearby. This somewhat dark spot might be lover's lane, but my fatigued leg muscles needed a break.

I leaned against the sweating surface and sighed with relief. The days I'd spent horizontal wouldn't have effected me this badly if I'd been exercising the past few months. My regime of walking home from the lab stalled when I started the drug testing. As soon as I got back to Earth I'd start running again. Running to my new job.

I'd finally found my true calling. I'd transfer to the bio-med group. They wouldn't refuse me, not when I knocked on their door with a product that was nearly ready to market. Before I handed it over, they'd have to agree that the majority of the profits went to cancer research. They'd balk at that, but wouldn't refuse. The creation of a drug like mine cost millions–and took years thanks to the bureaucracy–if done legally.

Plus, the next successful drug I developed would be all theirs. I ran through all the venoms I'd tested for tumor eradication and imagined their therapeutic and commercial uses. Why hadn't our groups collaborated sooner? A wall of snobbery separated our buildings. I'd break it down.

Only one thing nagged at me. Anton, Matthew and I all knew this drug made people feel good. Really good. While I intended it to be used before telling a patient they were terminal to prevent a drop in white blood cells, or after a traumatic event to prevent PTSD, pharmaceutical reps might have other ideas. I tried to set my worries aside. I had no control over regulation. The AGE had tough rules and smart staff, so I was confident this would be used as legitimately as any other drug.

I caught my breath–suddenly anxious–and the stars shifted. We'd just jumped. Victoria was smaller and slightly to the left.

I'd been so excited when I first saw this planet on the trip over. I'd used it as a lens to focus my hopes and dreams–and hadn't seen what I expected. Della and Jeremy had been reduced to little more than pixilated paper dolls, and my failures and latent talents had come into sharp focus.

I was nearsighted. I needed my family and goals right in front of me. Light-years away on Victoria it became clear that I could be a good father, if not to the right child, and that I didn't have the patience for pure research. My colleagues might mock me but I liked positive feedback, fast. As a biomedical engineer, I would see progress in a month instead of a decade. I wouldn't apologize for that anymore, and wouldn't have to once the credits started rolling in. We all had our strengths.

As the burst drive engines began their deep, rhythmic thrum in preparation for the next jump, my pang of regret for leaving Mia shifted to puzzlement. Who had I helped by stepping in as a surrogate parent? In the long view that Della favored, no one. I'd only helped by leaving. Matthew and Annette needed to focus on their daughter and my abrupt departure might prompt this.

I stood and dusted the crumbs from the front of my crinkly jumpsuit. The teen couple smiled and hurried to grab my spot. As I made my way back to my cabin through the happy sea of humanity, the heaviness I assumed was caused by Victoria's gravity finally lifted from my heart. I was going home.

M. Luke McDonell is a San Francisco-based writer and designer. Her near-future fiction explores the effects of technology on individuals and society, with particular focus on the growing power of corporations and the associated voluntary and involuntary loss of rights and privacy.

The Perfect Specimen is a prequel to her novel, Six.

Visit http://www.mlukemcdonell.com to learn more.

Follow @MLukeMc on Twitter for scintillating and informative tweets. :)

Thank you for reading!

The Perfect Specimen

CPSIA information can be obtained
at www.ICGtesting.com
Printed in the USA
FSHW010441101019
62851FS